W9-BVI-749

In The Course Of Two Short Weeks, She'd Reconnected With Rick, Found The Lover Of Her Dreams And Wound Up Pregnant.

Eileen remembered the look on Rick's face when she'd walked out of the office, leaving him alone. She'd seen the loneliness and resignation in his eyes, and had almost gone rushing back to him. Almost.

But she'd remembered the one important point.

He didn't want her for her.

He wanted her for the baby within her.

Disappointment welled up like a wave surging toward shore. Maybe if he'd proposed differently. Maybe if he'd told her that what they had was more than physical. Maybe if he'd—

A knock on the door had her jumping. *Rick?* Her stomach skittered nervously and she was torn between pleasure and impatience that he'd show up at the house to plead his case again. She didn't want to keep saying no, but she couldn't very well say yes to a man who didn't actually *want* her, could she?

Dear Reader,

Welcome to another stellar month of stories from Silhouette Desire. We kick things off with our DYNASTIES: THE BARONES series as Kristi Gold brings us *Expecting the Sheikh's Baby* in which—yes, you guessed it!—a certain long-lost Barone cousin finds herself expecting a very special delivery.

Also this month: The fabulous Peggy Moreland launches a brand-new series with THE TANNERS OF TEXAS, about *Five Brothers and a Baby,* which will give you the giddy-up you've been craving. The wonderful Brenda Jackson is back with another story about her Westmoreland family. *A Little Dare* is full of many big surprises…including a wonderful secret-child story line. And *Sleeping with the Boss* by Maureen Child will have you on the edge of your seat—or boardroom table, whatever the case may be.

KING OF HEARTS, a new miniseries by Katherine Garbera, launches with *In Bed with Beauty*. The series focuses on an angel with some crooked wings who must do a lot of matchmaking in order to secure his entrance through the pearly gates. And Laura Wright is back with *Ruling Passions,* a very sensual royal-themed tale.

So, get ready for some scintillating storytelling as you settle in for six wonderful novels. And next month, watch for Diana Palmer's *Man in Control*.

More passion to you!

Melissa Jeglinski

Melissa Jeglinski
Senior Editor, Silhouette Desire

Please address questions and book requests to:
Silhouette Reader Service
U.S.: 3010 Walden Ave., P.O. Box 1325, Buffalo, NY 14269
Canadian: P.O. Box 609, Fort Erie, Ont. L2A 5X3

Sleeping with the Boss

MAUREEN CHILD

Silhouette®

Desire

Published by Silhouette Books

America's Publisher of Contemporary Romance

If you purchased this book without a cover you should be aware
that this book is stolen property. It was reported as "unsold and
destroyed" to the publisher, and neither the author nor the
publisher has received any payment for this "stripped book."

 SILHOUETTE BOOKS

ISBN 0-373-76534-7

SLEEPING WITH THE BOSS

Copyright © 2003 by Maureen Child

All rights reserved. Except for use in any review, the reproduction
or utilization of this work in whole or in part in any form by any
electronic, mechanical or other means, now known or hereafter
invented, including xerography, photocopying and recording, or in
any information storage or retrieval system, is forbidden without
the written permission of the editorial office, Silhouette Books,
233 Broadway, New York, NY 10279 U.S.A.

All characters in this book have no existence outside the imagination of
the author and have no relation whatsoever to anyone bearing the same
name or names. They are not even distantly inspired by any individual
known or unknown to the author, and all incidents are pure invention.

This edition published by arrangement with Harlequin Books S.A.

® and TM are trademarks of Harlequin Books S.A., used under license.
Trademarks indicated with ® are registered in the United States Patent
and Trademark Office, the Canadian Trade Marks Office and in other
countries.

Visit Silhouette at www.eHarlequin.com

Printed in U.S.A.

Books by Maureen Child

Silhouette Desire

Have Bride, Need Groom #1059
*The Surprise Christmas
    Bride* #1112
Maternity Bride #1138
*The Littlest Marine #1167
**The Non-Commissioned
    Baby* #1174
*The Oldest Living Married Virgin #1180
*Colonel Daddy #1211
*Mom in Waiting #1234
*Marine under the Mistletoe #1258
*The Daddy Salute #1275
*The Last Santini Virgin #1312
*The Next Santini Bride #1317
*Marooned with a Marine #1325
*Prince Charming in Dress Blues #1366
*His Baby! #1377
*The Last Virgin in California #1398
Did You Say Twins?! #1408
The SEAL's Surrender #1431
*The Marine & the Debutante #1443
The Royal Treatment #1468
Kiss Me, Cowboy! #1490
Beauty & the Blue Angel #1514
Sleeping with the Boss #1534

Silhouette Books

Love Is Murder
    "In Too Deep"

Harlequin Historicals

Shotgun Grooms #575
    "Jackson's Mail-Order Bride"

*Bachelor Battalion

MAUREEN CHILD

is a California native who loves to travel. Every chance they get, she and her husband are taking off on another research trip. The author of more than sixty books, Maureen loves a happy ending and still swears that she has the best job in the world. She lives in Southern California with her husband, two children and a golden retriever with delusions of grandeur.

Visit her Web site at www.maureenchild.com.

To Wendi Heard Muhlenbruch—
an artist with flowers and the inspiration behind Eileen—
may your new baby bring you and Daren joy always.

One

Eileen Ryan faced her grandmother down in battle, even knowing that she would, eventually, lose the war. It was inevitable. Her grandmother was undefeated. If she wanted something, Margaret Mary—Maggie to her friends—Ryan, usually found a way to get it. But Eileen was determined to stand her ground. "Gran, I'm not a secretary anymore."

Sunlight danced in the small living room. The tiny beach cottage that Maggie Ryan had called home for more than forty years was packed full of her memories, but was never less than tidy. Gran sat in a splash of sunshine that gilded her perfectly styled gray hair. The older woman wore a pale peach dress, nylons and sensible black shoes. Her deeply lined features creased in a patient smile and her hands rested on the doily-covered arms of her favorite chair. She looked quietly regal—which was one of the reasons *no one* ever won an argument with her.

"Yes, but it's like riding a bike," Gran countered. "You never forget."

"You can if you work at it hard enough," Eileen told her, stubbornly clinging to her argument.

Heaven knows Eileen had certainly tried to forget everything about being a secretary. It had been three years since she'd last worked in an office. And she didn't miss it.

She'd always hated working in offices. First, there was the whole "trapped behind a desk" feeling—not to mention having to put up with a boss looking over your shoulder all the time. But the absolute worst part of being a secretary, as far as Eileen was concerned, was being smarter than the boss and having him treat her like an idiot. An old echo of pain welled up inside her and she fought it back down. Her last boss, Joshua Payton, had pretended to love her. Pretended to need her. Until he got the fat promotion that had taken him up the ladder of success and sent her back to the secretarial pool.

Well, she wouldn't be used and discarded again. She'd made her escape and didn't want to go back. Not even temporarily.

"Piffle."

"Piffle?" Eileen repeated, laughing.

Maggie's nose twitched. "It's not as though I were asking you to take a nosedive into the black hole of Calcutta."

"Close, though."

"I'm only asking you to help Rick out for two weeks. His secretary's gone on maternity leave and—"

"No way, Gran," she said, shaking her head and taking a step backward, just for good measure. Going into an office again was going backward. Revisiting a past that she'd just as soon forget.

Maggie didn't even blink. She simply stared at Eileen through emerald-green eyes and waited. And waited.

Eileen folded. She never had been able to stand tough under the silent treatment. "Come on, Gran. It's my vacation."

"Your vacation was canceled."

True. She and her best friend, Tina, had planned on two weeks in Mexico. Until, that is, Tina had unexpectedly eloped with her longtime boyfriend, leaving Eileen an apologetic message on her machine. Now Eileen had her passport in hand and no real desire to go to a fun-in-the-sun spot all on her lonesome.

Frustrating, since she'd spent so much time arranging things so that her flower shop wouldn't fold in her absence. Eileen had prepped her staff, coached her assistant and cleared her own decks to allow herself two whole weeks of a well-earned vacation. Early October was the best possible chance for her to take some time off. There was a real lull in a florist's calendar at this time of year—and as soon as October was finished, the holiday frenzy would kick in. She wouldn't have a moment to herself until after Valentine's Day.

Stress rattled through her like a freight train and even her eyes suddenly hurt. She could almost feel her time off slipping away from her. "The *trip* was canceled. I still have my two weeks."

"And nothing to do," her grandmother pointed out.

True again and darn it, Gran knew her *way* too well. Yes, she'd probably go a little nuts with nothing to occupy her time. But she was willing to risk it. "Hey, you never know. I might actually learn to *like* doing nothing at all."

Maggie chuckled. "Not you, honey. You never were one to sit still when you could be up and running."

"Maybe it's time I slowed down a little then," Eileen said, and started pacing. "I could read. Or go to the movies. Or maybe sit down at the beach and watch the waves."

Maggie waved a hand at her. "You wouldn't last twenty-four hours."

Eileen tried to placate her grandmother even while sticking to her plan to escape doing her this "favor." "Rick Hawkins is a pain, Gran, and you know it."

"You only say that because he used to tease you."

Eileen nodded. "You bet. Every time he came over to pick up Bridie for a date, he tormented me. He used to make me so mad."

"You were a little girl and he was your big sister's boyfriend. He was supposed to tease you. It was sort of his job."

"Uh-huh."

Maggie's sharp green eyes narrowed. "His grandmother is a very old, very dear friend."

"Great," Eileen interrupted in a rush. "I'll go help *her,* then."

"Nice try, but Loretta doesn't need a secretary. Her grandson *does.*"

"So what's he do, anyway?" Eileen plopped down into a chair close to her grandmother's. "With as mean as he was to me, I'm figuring he's some sort of criminal mastermind."

"Financial advisor," Maggie said, reaching up to tuck a stray curl behind her ear. "He's doing very well, too, according to Loretta."

Eileen wasn't impressed. "She's his grandmother. She's deluded, poor woman."

"Eileen…"

"Fine. So he's rich. Is he on wife number five by now?"

"Awfully curious, aren't you?"

"It's a tragic flaw."

Maggie's mouth twitched. "One ex-wife, no children. Apparently the woman was just a barracuda."

"Hey, even a barracuda doesn't stand a chance against a great white." She hated to admit that she felt even the slightest pang of sympathy for a guy she hadn't seen in years, but divorces were never pretty. Not that she would know from personal experience, of course. You had to actually get married to be able to experience divorce. And her one and only engagement had ended—thank heaven—before she'd actually taken the vows.

"Honestly, Eileen," her grandmother said. "You're making the man sound awful."

"Well…"

Maggie frowned at her. "Rick is the grandson of my very dear friend."

The solid steel guilt trap was swinging closed. Eileen could actually feel its cold, sharp jaws pinching at her flesh. Yet still she struggled. "Rick never liked me much either, you know."

"Don't be silly."

"He probably wouldn't *want* me to help him."

"Loretta says he's grateful for your offer."

Eileen's eyes bugged out. She wouldn't have been surprised to feel them pop right out of her head. "He *knows* already?" So much for free will.

"Well, I had to say something, didn't I?"

"And volunteering me was the first thing that came to mind?" Her only family, turning on her like a snake.

"You're a good girl, Eileen. I didn't think you'd mind."

"Rick Hawkins," she muttered, shaking her head. She hadn't seen him in six years. He'd come to her grandfather's funeral. Six years was a long time. And that was okay by her. The one brief glimpse of him in a business suit didn't wipe away her real memories of him. The way she remembered it, he was a bully who'd picked on an eleven-year-old kid who'd kinda, sorta, had a crush on him. There's a guy she wanted to work for. Nope. No way. Uh-uh. "I'm so not gonna do this."

Maggie Ryan rested her elbows on the arms of the floral tapestry chair and steepled her fingers. Tipping her head to one side, she studied her granddaughter and said softly, "When you were ten years old, you broke Great Grandmother O'Hara's china cup."

"Oh, God…" *Run, Eileen,* she told herself. *Run and keep on running.*

"I seem to remember you saying something along the lines of, 'I'm so sorry, Gran. I'll do anything to make it up to you. Anything.'"

"I was ten," Eileen protested, desperately looking for a loophole. "That was seventeen years ago."

Maggie sighed dramatically and laid one hand across what she was pretending to be a broken heart. "So, there's a time limit on promises in this house, is there?"

"No, but…" The trap tightened a notch or two. It was getting harder to breathe.

"That was the last cup in the set my grandmother carried over from the old country."

"Gran…" The cold, cold steel of guilt wrapped around her, the jaws of the trap nearly closed around her now. She winced.

The older woman rolled her eyes toward heaven. "*Her* grandmother gave her the set as a wedding gift. So she could bring it with her from County

Mayo—a piece of her old world. And she took it with love, knowing they'd never meet again in this life.''

If she started talking about the steerage section of the boat again, it was all over. "I know, but—"

"She kept those cups safe on the boat. It wasn't easy. She was in steerage, you know and—"

Snap.

"I surrender," Eileen said, lifting both hands in the traditional pose. No matter how much she wanted to avoid working for Rick, she was caught and she knew it. "I'll do it. I'll work for Rick. But it's two weeks only. Not a day longer."

"Wonderful, dear." Gran reached for the shamrock-dusted teacup on the table beside her. "Be at the office at eight tomorrow morning. I told Rick to expect you."

"You knew I'd do it all along, didn't you?"

Gran smiled.

"Just so you know, I still haven't forgiven you for the whole Barbie episode."

Rick Hawkins just stared at the tall, elegant-looking redhead standing in his outer office. Her features were wary, but couldn't disguise her beauty. Irish green eyes narrowed, but not enough to hide the gleam in their depths. Her mouth was full and lush, her eyebrows finely arched. Her hair fell in red-gold waves to her shoulders. She wore a white dress shirt tucked into sleek black slacks and shiny black boots peeked out from beneath the hem. Small silver hoops dangled from her ears and a serviceable silver watch encircled her left wrist. Her hands were bare but for a coat of clear nail polish. She looked businesslike. Dignified and too damn good.

He never should have listened to his grandmother. This could be a long two weeks.

"You were eleven," he reminded her at last.

"And you were almost sixteen," she countered.

"You were a pest." Looking at her now, though, he couldn't imagine being bothered by having her around. Which worried him a little. He'd been taken in by a gorgeous face before. He'd trusted her. Believed in her. And then she'd left. Just like every other woman in his life—except the grandmother who'd raised him after his mother decided she'd rather be a free spirit than be tied to a child.

She nodded, allowing his point. "True. But you didn't have to decapitate Barbie."

He smiled despite the memories crowding his brain. "Maybe not, but you left me alone after that."

"Well yeah." She folded her arms across her chest and tapped the toe of one shoe against the steel-blue carpet. "That's a sure sign of a serial killer in the making."

"Sorry to disappoint you. No grisly past here. Just a businessman."

She shrugged. "Same difference."

Rick shook his head. She had the same temperament she'd had as a kid. Always ready for war. Must be the red hair. And with a personality like that, this might just work. "Is the office going to be a war zone for the next two weeks, because if it is…"

"No," she said, tossing her black leather purse onto the desk that would be hers as long as she was there. "I'm just being pissy. It's not even your fault."

"For which I'm grateful."

"Cute."

"Peace, okay? I appreciate you helping me out, Eileen." He did. He needed the help. He just didn't need the kind of distraction she was no doubt going to be.

Her eyebrows went high on her forehead. "Hey," she said smiling, "that's an improvement. At least you didn't call me Eyeball."

"No," he said, giving her a slow, approving up-and-down look. The scrawny little girl with long braids and a perpetual scab on her knee was gone. This woman was a world away from the child he'd nicknamed Eyeball. "You're definitely an 'Eileen' these days."

She inclined her head in a silent thank-you and it seemed, he thought, that a temporary truce had been declared.

"It's been awhile," she said.

"Yeah." It had, in fact, been about six years since he'd last seen her. When they were growing up, he and the Ryan sisters had been thrown together a lot, thanks to their grandmothers' close friendship. But once out of high school—hell, once he and Eileen's sister Bridget had broken up, he'd stopped coming around.

And while he'd been gone, Eileen Ryan had done a hell of a job of growing up.

Damn it.

"How's your grandmother?" he asked.

"Just as spry and manipulative as always," Eileen said with a quick grin that dazzled him even from across the room. "Here I stand as living proof. Gran is probably the only woman in the world who could have talked me into taking on a job on what should have been my vacation."

"She's good."

"She is." She reached up to push her hair behind her ears. The silver hoops winked at him in the sunlight. "And she misses you. You should stop and see her sometime."

"I will," he said, meaning it. Maggie Ryan had been a second grandmother to him. It shamed him to admit that he hadn't kept up with her.

"How's your gran?"

"In Florida," he said, grinning. "To catch the space shuttle launch next week."

Eileen turned and leaned one hip on the edge of her desk. "She was always doing something exciting, as I remember it."

Rick smiled to himself. His grandmother had always been one for grand adventures. "I think she was actually born a gypsy and then sold to a normal family as a baby."

Eileen shrugged and that fabulous hair actually rippled with light and color. "What's normal?"

"Beats the hell outta me," he admitted. He'd once thought he knew what normal was. It was everything he didn't have. A regular family with a mom and a dad. A house with a picket fence and a big sloppy dog to play with. Dreams and plans and everything else he'd worked so hard to acquire. But now he wasn't so sure.

For some people, Rick thought, "normal" just never came into play. And that was okay with him now that he'd come to grips with the fact that he was a member of that particular group. He'd tried to find that normalcy once. He'd married a woman he thought loved him as much as he cared for her. By the time he'd figured out how wrong he was, she'd left, taking half of his business with her.

And his ability to trust went with her.

"So." Eileen's voice cut into his thoughts and he turned his attention back to her, gratefully. "What exactly is it you need me to do?"

"Right." Good idea, he told himself. Stick to business here. Just because their families were friendly was no reason for them to treat this situation as anything more than strictly business. Better all the way around, he thought as his gaze slipped back to her and he felt his blood thicken. Yep. A long two weeks.

Rick walked to the desk and stopped behind it. "Mainly, I need you to take care of the phones, take messages and type up a few reports for me when necessary.''

''So basically, you want me to stick my finger in a dyke and keep the place from flooding until you can get someone in here permanently.''

''Well, yeah, that's one way to put it.'' Rick pushed the edges of his navy-blue suit jacket back and shoved his hands into his pants pockets. ''With Margo out early on maternity leave, the place is falling apart and the temp agency can't send me anyone for another two weeks at least.''

''Whoa—'' Eileen held up one hand as she stared at him. Okay, she could admit, to herself anyway, that Rick Hawkins was a little…*more* than she'd expected. For some reason, even after that glimpse of him six years ago her mind had kept his image as he was at sixteen. Tall and lanky, with messy brown hair and a crooked smile. Well, that smile was there, but he wasn't lanky anymore. He was built like a man who knew what the inside of a gym looked like.

And his voice sounded like melted chocolate tasted.

So sure, she was female enough to be distracted. A lot. Until he'd used the words ''at least''. She wasn't about to let herself get sucked into giving him more than the agreed-on time.

''At least?'' she repeated. ''I can only do this for two weeks, Rick. Then I turn back into a pumpkin and head back out to Larkspur.''

''Larkspur?''

"My shop." Her pride and joy. The spot she'd worked so hard to build.

"Oh that's right. Grandma said you worked at a flower shop."

"I *own* a flower shop. Small, exclusive, with an emphasis on design." She reached across the desk for her purse, rummaged in its depths for a second or two, then came up with a brass card case. Flipping it open, she pulled out a card and handed it to him. Pale blue linen, the card stock was heavy, and the printing was embossed. A lone stalk of delicate-looking flowers curled around the left-hand side, looping around the name Larkspur. Eileen's name and phone number were discreetly added at the bottom.

"Very nice," Rick said, lifting his gaze back to hers as he automatically tucked the card into his breast pocket.

"Thanks. We do good work. You should give us a try."

"I will." A heartbeat or two passed and the silence in the room dragged on, getting thicker, heavier, warmer. Something indefinable sizzled in the air between them and Rick told himself to put a lid on it. He'd never made a play for a co-worker before and *now* certainly wasn't the time to start. Not when he would have *two* grandmothers out for his head if Eileen complained.

"Anyway," he said, his voice a little louder than he'd planned, "two weeks will be great. I'm sure the temp agency will come through for me."

"There're plenty of temp agencies out there. Why not try a different one?"

He shook his head. "I've tried lots of them. *This* one always sends good people. Most of them don't. I'd rather wait."

"Why didn't you get someone lined up before Margo left?"

"Good question," he said wryly. "Should have. But I was so busy trying to get things done and finished before she was gone, that time sort of got away from me. And then in the last month or so, Margo wasn't her usual organized self."

"She probably had more important things on her mind."

"I suppose." His trusty secretary-assistant had left him high and dry even before her last day of work. Margo's normally brilliant brain had dissolved into a sea of pregnancy hormones and daydreams of pitter-pattering feet. He couldn't wait for her to give birth so things could get back to normal. "I'm just glad she's going to come back to work after she has the kid."

"That's a shame," Eileen said.

"Huh?" He looked at her. "Why?"

"Well, because if I had a baby, I'd want to be able to stay home and take care of it myself." Eileen set her purse down again, walked around the edge of the desk and nudged him out of the way so she could sit down in the blue leather desk chair. "I mean, I know lots of women *have* to work, but if you don't have to…"

"Margo would go nuts without something to do with her day," he argued, recalling his secretary's gung-ho attitude. "She likes being busy."

"I hear babies can keep you plenty busy."

He shuddered at the thought of Margo turning into a stay-at-home mom. "Don't say that. She *has* to come back to work. She runs this place."

"She probably will then," Eileen said and opened the top drawer, inspecting, looking around, familiarizing herself with the setup. "I'm just saying…"

"Don't say it again. You'll jinx it."

"Very mature." She shut the drawer and opened another one, poking through the pads and boxes of pencils and even a bag of candy Margo had left behind. Pulling one piece free, she peeled off the silver foil and popped the chocolate into her mouth. "Do we have a coffee pot?"

"Right over there." He pointed, looking away to keep from noticing how her tongue swept across her bottom lip as she chased every last crumb of chocolate.

"Thank God," she muttered, and hopped up again. Striding across the room to the low oak sideboard, she glanced over her shoulder at him. "Since it's my first day, I'll even get you a cup. After that though, you're on your own. I'm not a waitress. I'm a secretary. Temporarily."

Temporarily, he reminded himself as his gaze locked onto the curve of her behind as she moved with an easy sway that was enough to knock any man's temperature up a notch or two. Hell, every relationship became temporary eventually. At least this one was labeled correctly right from the start.

This could only be trouble, he told himself and wondered how in the hell he'd survive the next two weeks with Eileen back in his life.

By day three, Eileen remembered exactly why she'd left the business world for that of flowers. Flowers never gave you a headache. Flowers didn't expect you to have all the answers. Flowers didn't look great in three-piece suits.

Okay, that last one wasn't one of her original reasons for relinquishing her keyboard. But it was right up there on the list now.

The work wasn't hard. It was actually fairly interesting, though she'd never admit that out loud to Rick. And, after spending the past two years in a work wardrobe that consisted of jeans and a wide selection of T-shirts, it was sort of nice getting dressed up again. Good thing she hadn't gotten rid of her work wardrobe. Slacks, shirts, discreet pumps or her comfy boots. She was wearing makeup and doing her hair every morning, too. A big change from her usual ponytail and a quick slash of lipstick. But none of that made up for the fact that she was spending way too much time watching Rick.

She'd had a crush on him when she was a kid, of course. Well, at least until the unfortunate Barbie incident. He and Bridie had ignored her most of the time and, when forced to spend time with her, Rick had teased Eileen until she'd wanted to kick him.

But now…she turned her head just far enough to be able to look into his office through the partially opened door.

With his tie loosened at his open collar and his dark brown hair mussed from stabbing his fingers through it in frustration, he looked…what was the word? Oh, yeah. *Tasty.*

Oh ye gods.

This was a complication she didn't want or need.

She couldn't be fantasizing about Rick Hawkins. For one thing, when these two weeks were up, she'd be going back to her world, leaving him to his and never their twain would meet again. For another…he was *so* not her type. She liked the artsy guys with a slightly bohemian air that she ran into down at the beach. The guys who were tanned and relaxed, with the attitude of *why do today what can be put off indefinitely?* Those guys were safe. She knew no relationship with them was going to go anywhere. The farthest they could see into the future was the next wave. Or their next paycheck. They didn't have portfolios.

Heck, most of them didn't own a pair of shoes that required socks.

So why suddenly was she spending way too much time thinking about, and fantasizing about, Mr. Corporate Millionaire?

Two

Rick leaned back in his chair and watched Eileen stop just at the threshold. She'd been doing that for three days now. She did the work. She was efficient, smart, organized. But she kept him at a distance. Always made sure she held herself back from him. And if he was smart, he'd appreciate that.

Instead, it frustrated him.

He hadn't expected to be so attracted to her. When his grandmother had first suggested Eileen as a temporary secretary, Rick hadn't been able to imagine it. The Eileen he'd known years ago was hardly his idea of a good assistant. But he'd been desperate and willing to try anything. Now that she was here, he could hardly think of anything else.

Probably not a good sign.

"Hello? Earth to Rick."

He blinked, coming up out of his thoughts like a man waking from a coma. "What?"

"I don't know. You called me in here, remember?" Eileen was still standing in the doorway, but now she was looking at him as if he had a screw loose. And hell. Maybe he did.

He pushed out of the chair and stood up. He'd always thought better on his feet anyway. "Yeah. I did. I'll need you to stay a little later tonight—" He broke off when the phone in the outer office rang.

"Hold that thought." Eileen turned and walked to her desk.

He deliberately avoided watching the sway of her hips. It wasn't easy.

She grabbed the receiver on the third ring. "Hawkins Financial."

Rick watched her as she reached across the desk for a pen. The hem of her skirt rode tantalizingly high on her thighs with the movement and he told himself not to look. But hell, he was male, right? And breathing? Impossible *not* to look.

Didn't mean a thing.

"Vanessa Taylor?" Eileen turned to glance at him, a question in her eyes.

Damn.

No, he mouthed, shaking his head and waving both hands. All he needed right now, was having to listen to Vanessa ramble about cocktail parties she wanted him to take her to. Never mind that he hadn't called her in weeks. Vanessa simply assumed that every man who crossed her path would become her helpless love slave. Rick Hawkins, however, didn't believe in love or slavery.

Tell her anything, he mouthed the instructions and hoped to hell Eileen was good at lipreading. He felt like a damn mime. But he couldn't risk a whisper. Vanessa had ears like a bat. She'd know he was there, then she'd insist on talking to him and he just wasn't interested.

Hell, he hadn't been interested when they *were* going out.

Anything? Eileen mouthed back, a decided gleam in her eyes. When he nodded, she smiled wickedly and said, "I'm sorry Ms. Taylor, but Rick can't come to the phone right now. The doctors have advised him to not speak until the stitches are gone."

What? Rick took a step closer.

Eileen backed up. "Oh, you didn't hear? A minor accident," she said, laughter in her eyes and feigned sympathy in her voice. "I'm sure the disfigurement won't be permanent." An instant later, Eileen jerked the phone from her ear and winced. "Wow. She slammed the phone down so hard I think I may be deaf."

Rick stared at her. "Disfigurement? I'm disfigured? Why did you do that?"

"Eh?" She cupped one hand around her ear and tilted her head.

"Funny, Ryan." He smirked at her. Pushing the edges of his jacket back, he shoved both hands into his pockets and rocked on his heels. "What's the deal?"

"You said I should tell her anything."

"Within reason."

She held up one finger and shook it. "No one said anything about reason."

Rick pulled his hands free of his pockets and crossed his arms over his chest. She kept surprising him. Which intrigued him. Which worried the hell out of him. "I didn't think I'd have to *request* reason. I'll be more prepared next time."

She chuckled.

"You enjoyed that."

"Oh yeah," she admitted, and leaned back, perching her behind on the edge of her desk. "And by the way, Vanessa?" She shook her head sadly. "Not the deepest puddle on the block. Just the word 'disfigurement' was enough to get rid of her." She studied him through amused eyes. "Swimming in pretty shallow pools, aren't you?"

Shallow? Good description of Vanessa and all of her pals. But hey, he wasn't interested in meaningful. At the time, all he'd been interested in was a dinner companion and a bed warmer. Vanessa hadn't been much good at either one. But that was hardly the point.

"Are you this mouthy with all of your employers?"

She came away from the desk. "I don't have an employer. Not anymore. I'm my own boss."

"Probably a wise move."

"What's that supposed to mean?"

"You don't play well with others, do you?"

"I've been doing a good job, haven't I?"

"Sure," Rick said, moving a little closer. Her scent reached out to him and he sucked it in. Stupid. "If you don't take into account the grumbling and the refusal to take orders and—"

"I don't need to follow orders, I know how to run an office—"

Hell, she was as easy to bait as she'd been as a kid. That Irish temper of hers was always bubbling and simmering just below the surface. And watching the temper flash in her eyes was damn near hypnotic. The emerald-green depths churned and darkened and bordered on dangerous, and still Rick was fascinated.

"But this is *my* office," he countered, egging her on. Her skin flushed, her breathing quickened and she looked like a coiled spring ready to explode. And his mouth nearly watered. Man, he was in some serious trouble here. He hadn't wanted a woman so badly in…ever.

"Oh, I know it's your office," she said, taking a step closer and leaning in for effect. "It's got your boring, unoriginal stamp all over it. Anyone else would have a little color around here. But not the great Rick Hawkins. Oh no. Let's play the corporate game. Battleship-gray all the way for you, isn't it? You're just one of the fleet. No originality at all."

"Originality?" She could say whatever the hell

she wanted about the decor. Because he couldn't
give a good damn about what the place looked like,
beyond it appearing dignified and successful. Did
she really think he was the kind of guy to carry
swatches of fabric around, for God's sake?

But he was damned if he'd stand here and be
called a lemming. He'd opened up more brokerage
accounts in the past year than any of his competitors.
He'd become the fastest growing firm on the West
Coast over the past three years and that hadn't happened because he blindly followed everyone else.

"Well, look around you," she exclaimed. "This
whole building is like a warren of rabbit holes. And
every one of you bunnies is tucked away in your
little gray worlds." She waved her hands around,
encompassing the pale gray walls, the steel-blue carpet and the generic watercolors dotted sparingly
throughout the room. "I'm willing to bet the same
interior decorator did *all* of the offices in this place.
You've probably all got the same awful paintings
hung in the same places on the same gray walls."

"Because I work in an office building I'm unoriginal?"

She nodded sharply. "Hard to be a free spirit
when you work on the *S.S. Conformity.*"

"What?" He had to laugh despite her insulting
tone. She was way over the top. Like some latter-
day hippie. He half expected her to start chanting
and calling on Sister Moon to help free his soul.

Damn, he hadn't had this much fun in a long time.

"What you need is—" She slapped one hand to her left eye and shouted, *"Freeze."*

"What?" Instinctively he took a step.

"Don't move." She gave him a one-eyed glare. "Don't you know what 'freeze' means?"

"What the hell are you talking about now?"

Slowly she lowered herself to the floor. "My contact. I lost a contact."

"You're kidding."

"Do I look like I'm kidding?" She tipped her head back to stare at him.

"You wear contact lenses?"

Her one good eye narrowed. The other was squeezed shut. "Well, to coin a phrase, *duh.*"

Rick glanced at the floor and carefully went down on his knees. "I knew your eyes couldn't be that green naturally."

"Watch where you kneel!" she blurted, then giving him a one eyed glare again, she added, "And they're not tinted lenses, if you must know."

He looked at her. "Prove it."

She opened her left eye. Just as green as the right one. Deep and pure and clear, they looked like the color of spring grass. Or, of a backlit emerald in a jeweler's display case. He stared into her eyes and, for a moment, let himself get lost in their depths. It was almost like drowning, he thought, then brought himself up short when she tore her gaze from his. He wasn't going to drown in any woman's eyes. Not again.

"So." She swallowed hard, inhaled quickly and said, "Just run your fingers gently over the carpet."

"This happen often?" he asked as he knelt beside her.

"Usually just when I'm upset."

"So, often."

She gave him an elbow to the ribs. "Cute."

"So I've been told."

"By Vanessa?" she asked.

"Vanessa was a client," he explained, his gaze searching the carpet as his fingers traced softly across the fabric. "We had dinner a couple of times, that's all."

"Apparently she's still hungry."

"Too bad," he muttered, briefly remembering just how boring Vanessa really was, "because I've had enough."

"Ooh." Eileen turned her head to look at him. "Sounds like there's a story there."

He glanced at her. She flipped her hair to one side. She smiled and something inside him tightened. Her fingers brushed his as they searched and he felt a short stab of heat that sliced right down to his insides. He'd never felt that with Vanessa. Or his ex-wife. Or anyone else for that matter.

Damn it, she was getting to him. And he couldn't allow that to happen. He had to remind himself that Eileen was just an old—not friend—not enemy, either. And certainly not old. So what did that make her? Besides, of course, a top-grade, A number-one temptation?

"Hello?" she muttered, and waved one hand in front of his face.

"Right. Story. No story. Vanessa was just…" He thought about it for a long moment. He didn't owe her or anyone else an explanation. But since she was staring at him from one good eye, he knew she wouldn't just drop it, either. Finally he said simply, "Temporary."

Her eyebrows arched. "Lot of that going around."

"Nothing lasts forever." His voice sounded tight, harsh, even to his own ears.

"Well, that's looking on the bright side." She crawled forward an inch or two.

"Just realistic." He knew that better than anyone. Love, friendship, relationships, they all ended. Usually when you were least expecting it. A long time ago Rick had decided to take charge of his world. Now *he* ended things before they got complicated. *He* was the one to walk away. He'd never be the one standing alone with a broken heart again.

Crawling carefully along the carpet, he stayed close to her. "How far can these things roll, anyway?"

"Pretty far," she said. "So, why is realistic cynical, why?"

He glanced at her. Damn, she was too close. Close enough that he could count the handful of freckles dusting the bridge of her nose. There were six. Not that he cared. "Why are you so interested?"

She shrugged. "Humor a half-blind woman."

Rick chuckled. She made him laugh. Had been since the first day she was here. And that was something he didn't do nearly often enough. He'd been too busy building his world to take the time to enjoy what he'd created. Too busy proving to everyone— including himself—that he *could* go to the top, to enjoy the trip. But somehow, Eileen lightened things up, even when she was arguing with him.

Impossible to ignore, too dangerous to pay attention to. Great combination.

He shrugged and stopped, thinking for a second he'd spotted a glint of light, like sunlight bouncing off a lens, but then it was gone. "No deep dark explanation," he said, refusing to be drawn into the long, sad history of his past relationships. Not only wasn't it any of Eileen's business, but he'd learned to let it go. No point in revisiting it. "Vanessa and I were just two ships colliding briefly in the night, then going our own way. That's realistic, not cynical. Pretending it was anything else would be a waste of time."

Colliding ships, huh? Eileen mused on his choice of words for a minute or two. If their ships had collided, then they'd probably slept together. Which meant this Vanessa had seen Rick naked. Instantly an image flashed into Eileen's mind. The same image that had been taunting her for the past few days.

She kept imagining Rick wet.

Stepping out of the shower, a skimpy towel wrapped around his waist, beads of water clinging to the hairs on his chest. Then she imagined him shaking his head and tiny droplets of water flying from the ends of his hair like diamonds. Then she imagined the towel dropping and him stepping forward to take her into his arms. The vision was so clear, so tantalizing, she could feel his wet skin next to hers. He bent his head, his mouth just a breath away from hers and then—

"Found it!"

She sucked in air like an old, wheezing vacuum. "What?"

"Your lens," Rick said, holding it out to her. "I found it."

"Right." She swallowed that gulp of air and held it in, hoping to steady herself. Jeez. Did it have to be so darn hot in the room? Right now, she felt as though a fever were racing through her body. She looked into his eyes, and those brown depths seemed to pull her in. His victorious grin set off a series of minor explosions within her and her blood pumped as if she was in the last leg of a marathon.

She'd never had this sort of reaction to a man before. Oh, the cute ones jangled her nerves, and here and there a fabulous mouth might make her a little antsy. But *never* had she fantasized so well that her whole body was tingling with heat and want.

Not even over her late, unlamented ex-fiancée. Not even with her last boss…the one with lots of promises and an exceptionally bad memory about them.

Nope. Rick stirred things up that had never been stirred before.

Oh, boy.

"Thanks," she said, and picked her contact lens up from the center of his palm. The brush of her fingertips against his skin sent another jagged spear of something dark and wicked through her body, but Eileen fought it. Otherwise, she'd be forced to roll over onto her back and shout, *Take me, big boy!*

Oh, wow.

Eileen pushed herself to her feet. "Okay, better go take care of this. Don't want to look at life like a Cyclops."

She headed unsteadily toward the door. He was right behind her, but Eileen didn't look back. The words "pillar of salt" kept reverberating inside her mind.

"Can I help?"

"No thanks," she said, waving one hand. "Been doing this for years."

"I didn't know you wore contacts."

"No reason you should, since we haven't seen each other in six years."

The hall looked impossibly long. The wall on her right was painted the ever-present gray, but the wall on her right was glass. Afternoon sunshine poured in, and five stories below them, it winked off the windshields of the cars jammed bumper to bumper on the 405 freeway. Just the thought of joining the thundering herd trying to get home made her grateful that Rick wanted her to stay later than usual.

Even if he was making her a little nervous.

"Man," Rick said from behind her, as if reading her mind, "the freeway's a mess."

"I noticed." She made a sharp right and walked into the ladies' room.

"It should be thinned out later, though. We could send out for dinner while we work."

Dinner. She wasn't sure she'd be able to swallow. Eileen looked into the mirror and stared at Rick's reflection. He was there. Right behind her. In the pale blue lounge area. Of the *ladies'* room, for Pete's sake. Two vinyl chairs sat on either side of a low table holding a bowl of fresh flowers. Eileen looked into the mirror, ignoring the furnishings to stare instead at Rick. "Dinner?"

"What? You don't eat?"

"Sure I eat. I just usually don't have men following me into the ladies' room to deliver an invitation."

He shifted his gaze from hers and looked around, as if surprised to discover where he was. Then he looked back into the mirror, meeting her gaze again with a wry, crooked smile. "Oops."

Eileen felt a *ping* bounce around inside her and realized that smile of his could still affect her. Apparently, at heart, she was still that eleven-year-old girl with a kinda sorta crush. For heaven's sake.

He jerked a thumb at the closed door behind him. "I'll, uh, see you outside."

"Good idea."

Once he was gone, Eileen let out a breath she hadn't realized she was holding. Leaning forward, she planted both hands on the slate-blue Formica counter and stared at her reflection. ''This temporary job was a *bad* idea, Eileen. *Really* bad.''

Three

Rick hadn't had Mexican fast food in far too long. He didn't remember tacos and nachos ever tasting quite so good. And he'd never considered having an indoor picnic on the floor of his office. But then maybe it wasn't the food, he told himself. Maybe it was sharing it with Eileen. She was annoying, irritating and more entertaining than he would have guessed.

Watching her now while she talked about some of her customers, he saw her eyes flash with humor.

"This one guy is a regular," she was saying, and paused to take a small bite of a taco. She chewed, swallowed and said, "He's got a standing order for a dozen roses once a week."

"Good husband?" Rick ventured.

"Hardly," she said with a quick shake of her head. "It's for the girl of the week. Always someone different, always a different color rose—according to their personalities, he says. But one week, he changed the order—switched to a spider plant."

One of Rick's eyebrows lifted. "Makes you wonder, doesn't it?"

"Makes me wonder how he finds so many women willing to go out with him." She sighed and leaned back, bracing her hands on the floor behind her. "His bedroom must be like an assembly line."

"And you think I'm cynical?" Rick drew one knee up and rested his forearm on top.

"Touché." She inclined her head at him, allowing him a point.

"So," he asked after a long minute of silence, "how's Bridie doing?"

Eileen smiled. "Big sister's doing fine," she said, thinking about Bridget and her ever-growing family. "Three and a half kids and a husband she drools over. She's disgustingly happy."

"Three and a half?"

"Pregnant again," she said with a slow shake of her head. "Hard to imagine, but Bridie just loves being pregnant and Jefferson—that's her husband—he's as nuts about kids as she is." Eileen met Rick's gaze. "If you guys hadn't split up, you could have been a very busy father by now."

He frowned, reached for his soda and took a long drink. "No, thanks." He set the large cup back onto the rug. "Tried the husband thing. It didn't work. Besides, I'm not father material."

"There's that sunshiny outlook on life I've come to know so well," Eileen said.

"Touché." His turn to incline his head and acknowledge her point. Then he asked, "What about you?"

"What about me?"

"You involved with anyone?" And why do you care? Rick asked himself. The answer was, he didn't. Not really. It was just a polite inquiry. Didn't matter to him one way or the other.

She sat up, dusted her palms together and gathered up her trash, stuffing it into the white paper bag. "Not lately."

Good, he thought even though he knew it would have been better if she were engaged. Married. Hell. A nun. "Hard to believe."

"Why?" She looked up at him.

He shrugged. "It's just…" He waved a hand at her. "I mean…"

She smiled. "Are you about to give me a compliment?"

Frowning, Rick crumpled up the last of his trash and snatched the bag from her hand to stuff his trash inside. "Stranger things have happened."

"In science fiction movies."

"You're not an easy person, are you, Eyeball?"

She tossed a wadded-up taco wrapper at him, bouncing it off his forehead. "Gran always said nothing good ever comes easy."

"Yeah, but who knew she was talking about you?"

Silence dropped between them. Outside the windows, the sun was setting and the low-lying clouds were shaded a deep purple and crimson. And inside, the silence kept growing, until it was a living, breathing presence in the room.

Rick stared at her and caught himself wondering what she would taste like. And he wondered if he'd be willing to stop at just one taste. That couldn't happen though. He wouldn't get involved with Eileen Ryan. Beyond the fact that she aroused too much emotion within him—there was the whole business of her being the granddaughter of his grandmother's best friend.

She wasn't the woman for a no-strings affair. She was hearth and home and family dinners. Definitely, she was *hands off*. There might as well have been a sign reading Keep Away tacked to her forehead.

If he was smart, he'd pay attention.

"We'd better finish up that contract stuff," she said, her gaze locked with his.

"Right." Rick nodded and pulled in a deep breath. "Otherwise, we could be here all night."

"Probably not a good idea," Eileen said softly, and licked her lips.

"Yeah," he said, wincing as his body tightened. "Not a good idea at all."

By Thursday evening, Eileen was regretting ever agreeing to this situation. She felt as if she was tightrope walking over a pit filled with hungry lions. One wrong step and she was nothing more than a quick meal.

What she needed was the weekend. Time to spend down at the beach, in her own cottage. Painting the china hutch she'd picked up at the flea market last month. Or stenciling the kitchen walls. Heaven knows, she'd been putting that off for months. There'd never been enough time to get around to all of the crafty things she liked to do. She was always too busy at the shop.

Which was why she'd been looking forward to these two weeks. With Paula, her new manager, in charge at Larkspur, Eileen could relax about the shop. It was in good hands.

Her full vacation was already shot, so she planned to make good use of at least the weekends. She'd have some breathing room. She needed to get herself far, far away from Rick Hawkins. She needed to keep busy enough that maybe she'd stop daydreaming about what she'd like to be doing with Rick. Eileen groaned quietly. All she had to do was get through today and tomorrow, and she'd have two whole days to decompress.

"Eileen?"

"Yessir, boss?" She turned her head to watch him come through the doorway from his office.

He frowned and looked at her as she stood up, holding onto her purse and car keys as if they were life rings tossed into a churning sea. "You leaving already?"

"It's not 'already,'" she said, scooping her black cardigan off the back of her chair. "It's after five and I'm going home." She was actually *running* home, but didn't feel the urge to tell him that. Back to her empty little cottage where she wouldn't have to look into Rick's brown eyes. Where she wouldn't have to remind herself that she wasn't interested in getting involved with *anyone* again, much less the bane of her childhood.

Slipping into her sweater, she flipped her hair out from under it, then pointed at a manila folder on her desk. "The last letters you wanted are right there. Sign them and they'll go out in tomorrow morning's mail."

"Fine, but—"

"See you later."

"Eileen."

His voice stopped her just three feet from the door. She gave that magic portal one longing glance, then took a deep breath and turned to face him. His hair was mussed, his tie loose and his collar opened. He looked far too good. If he suggested ordering dinner in and working late again, she'd have to say yes. She'd spend the whole meal drooling over him and then go home to be frustrated alone. But if he didn't ask her to stay late and have dinner, she'd be disappointed because then she wouldn't get a chance to drool over him. Oh yeah. No psychological problems *here*. "What?" She snapped out the word a little harsher than she'd planned.

"You free this weekend?"

Whoa. She reeled a little. Was he asking her what she thought he might be asking her? Not just fast-food dinner and work, but maybe a date? Maybe a movie or something else that was totally inappropriate considering they were working together? Considering their *grandmothers* had arranged all of this? Considering that she wasn't in the mood for a man in her life? Ye gods. Her stomach skittered nervously. "Why?"

"I've got some meetings."

Okay, no date. Work.

"Now that's a shame," she said, and sidled closer to the door.

"I'll need a secretary."

No way. She'd already lost two perfectly good weeks of vacation. She wasn't about to give up her weekends, too. "Rick…"

"One meeting's scheduled for late tomorrow morning, then all day Saturday. Maybe one Sunday morning."

"But I don't—"

"You'll be paid overtime."

Her fingers curled around her purse strap. "That's not the point."

"What is?" he asked, folding his arms across a chest that she'd spent far too much time imagining bare. "Too scared to go away with me?"

She laughed shortly, harshly and hoped it sounded convincing. "Yeah. That must be it—go away? Go away where?"

"Temecula."

"In Riverside county?"

"Is there another one?"

"No, but—"

Rick walked across the room, stared out the window for a long minute, then turned to look at her again. "Edward Harrington was my first client when I opened my business." Rick shrugged. "He took a chance on me. Twice a year, I go out to Riverside to look over his portfolio and discuss changes and investments."

"You go to him?"

Rick smiled. "Most independents go to their customers."

"Still. One customer's going to take all weekend?"

"No, but Edward referred me to some of his golf buddies and I see *all* of them when I go out there. I'm seeing Edward tomorrow and then the others on Saturday."

"So you work all week and then even more on the weekend."

"Uh-huh." He studied her for a long, thoughtful minute, unfolded his arms, then waved both hands at her. "You know what? Never mind. You're right."

Wary now, Eileen watched him. It wasn't like him to change tactics so suddenly. "I'm right about what?"

"I can't ask you to go."

"You already did," she pointed out.

"I take it back."

"What?" she said. Turning around, he walked back into his office. She was right behind him. Rick smiled at her hurried footsteps as she raced to catch up. "You take it back?" she asked. "What are you, in third grade?"

"Nope." He walked around behind his desk and took a seat. Keeping his gaze averted from hers, Rick shuffled through the piles of financial reports on his desk. The minute he'd asked her to go along, he'd known she'd refuse. And maybe that was how he should leave it. It'd be a hell of a lot safer. But damn it, he wanted her to go with him. Wanted her away from the office and on neutral territory. Wanted her—hell.

He just wanted her. "I'm just being logical," he said. "I can handle the work without you. And you'd hate it anyway and I don't blame you. You'd be bored."

"Bored?"

"Sure." He glanced at her. Her eyes were flashing. It was working. Damn, she hadn't changed a bit. For one brief second, he wished he'd been wrong and that she had simply said, *Okay fine. See you.* Then that feeling was gone and he was prodding her again. "Besides, like I said, I can handle this alone. I'll take a laptop with me. Type up my own notes."

She snorted.

He glanced at her. "I don't need a secretary after all," he went on, warming to his theme now that he was on a roll. Eileen was reacting just as he'd known she would. Just as she always had. Tell her she couldn't do something and there was nothing she wanted to do more. Like the time when she was ten and her gran told her that she couldn't hang on to a car bumper while on her skateboard. Naturally, she'd done it anyway, the car made a sharp right turn and Eileen had broken her wrist when she crashed into Mrs. Murphy's trash cans.

Maybe it was a mistake to challenge her hard enough so that she would come along for the weekend, but damned if he could resist the idea. He hadn't felt this kind of attraction for a woman before. And it was bloody hard to deny it.

Her green eyes were stormy and he could actually *see* thoughts and emotions pinwheeling through her mind. God, she was so easy to read. And he enjoyed it after years of looking at a woman and wondering just what the hell she was thinking behind her cool, polite mask of interest.

"You don't need a secretary?" she said. "You, who types with two fingers?"

One eyebrow lifted. "Speed won't be required. Just accuracy."

She frowned at him, turning that delicious-looking mouth into a pout that made him want to bite her. Oh yeah, it'd be much better—safer—if she told him no. Damn, he hoped she didn't. "I can handle note taking. I'll bring a tape recorder or something. You can type everything up on Monday."

"I could go with you."

"Well, of course you *could,*" Rick said, watching her as she leaned both hands on the front of his desk. The high collar of her business shirt dipped just a bit and he caught a tantalizingly small peek at her chest. But just that tiny glimpse was enough to make him hard—and damn grateful to be sitting behind his desk. Clearing his throat, he continued, "I'm just saying, there's no reason to. I wouldn't want to put you out."

She pushed up from the desk, planted both hands at her hips and countered, "I'm working for you. It's part of the job."

"I can't ask you to go away with me for the weekend." He kept arguing, knowing it was in her nature to dig in her heels. She was absolutely the most contrary woman he'd ever met. She fascinated him. "Wouldn't be fair."

"Fair?" she repeated. "Now we're talking about fair?"

"Hey." Rick leaned back in his chair, gripped the arms and said, "I'm only trying to be reasonable."

"Uh-huh. Where's the meeting?" she asked, tapping the toe of one shoe against the carpet with a staccato beat.

He hid a smile at the temper already rising inside her. He should feel guilty about manipulating her into this, but he didn't. "Eileen, it's not necessary for you to go."

"I'm *going.*" She glared at him. "I'm your secretary and it's my job."

"I don't think it's a good idea."

"Deal with it," she said. "Honestly, you wanted me to work for you and then when I say I am, you say no."

"Just trying to be fair."

"Well, quit it."

"Okay." He held up both hands and surrendered. "Didn't know it would mean this much to you."

"Now you know."

"I appreciate it."

"No problem." She inhaled sharply and blew it out again in a rush. "Where do you want me to make reservations?"

"The Hammond Inn will work. Their number's in the Rolodex."

"Fine," she said, and turned to leave the room.

"Get a two-bedroom suite. We can work in the living area."

Eileen stopped and looked back over her shoulder at him. His brown eyes looked rich and dark and impossibly deep. Her insides twisted suddenly and she heard herself say, "I'm not going to sleep with you, you know."

His eyes narrowed. "Don't recall asking you to."

"Okay then." She blew out a breath and nodded sharply. "Just so we're clear."

"Crystal."

She left his office and closed the door behind her. Then she leaned back against it and stared blankly at the ceiling. "What happened?" she whispered aloud. "You just gave away your weekend. What were you thinking?" She'd practically begged him to let her go along. And worse yet, now she'd be sharing a suite with the very man she was trying to stay away from.

"Yeah, you're doing great, Eileen," she told herself and headed for her desk. She had to make the reservation before leaving for the day. Sending the Rolodex into a wild spin, she muttered, "Just great."

The Hammond Inn was the perfect romantic getaway. An hour and a half away from Orange County by freeway, it was a world away in feeling. The town of Temecula had started life as a stagecoach stop...and was now an interesting collection of old and new.

Many of the original buildings were still standing in old town, but the new housing developments were springing up all over everywhere like a virus run amok. Still, there were ranches and elegant old homes studding the landscape and the Hammond Inn was a perfect example.

A gracious Victorian, it had been perfectly restored to its former glory. Its wraparound porch was studded with hand-carved pillars painted a pristine white. The house itself was bright, sunshine-yellow with white trim and dark green shutters. The wide porch held clusters of white wicker furniture, inviting cozy conversations. Hanging plants hung from the overhanging roof, dotting the porch with thick green foliage. Late-blooming chrysanthemums burst into rainbows of color along the skirt of the house and lined the long walkway from the curved drive-way. Maples and oaks, now boasting their brilliant fall colors, crouched around the house like protective soldiers decked out in their dress uniforms.

A cold wind swept through the hills, rattled the leaves and bowed the flowers as Eileen and Rick walked up the path.

"It's gorgeous," she said, turning around to get the whole picture. Trees dotted the rolling, winter-brown hills and though new housing developments were encroaching, they were still far enough away that the inn seemed secluded. Private.

Eileen shot Rick a sidelong glance and told herself to get a grip. They weren't here for romance. The inn was simply a temporary headquarters. They were here to conduct meetings with a few of Rick's clients. They all lived locally and it was much easier for Rick and her to spend the weekend at the inn rather than driving the freeway to Riverside County every day.

Although, she thought, turning back around to continue walking, if they *had* been here for romance, they couldn't have picked a better spot.

"I like it," Rick said, oblivious, thank heaven, to her thoughts. "The owners aren't the kind to organize 'fun' for their guests. They leave me alone to conduct business."

Eileen shot him a look and shook her head. "Get down, you funky party weasel."

He stopped and gave her that look she was becoming all too accustomed to. It was the sort of stare you gave someone speaking a foreign language. Conveying the thought that maybe, if you listened hard enough, you'd understand. "Party weasel?"

"*Funky* party weasel. That was sarcasm."

"Thought it might be."

Eileen waved one hand up and down in front of him. "But honestly, Rick. Look at you. You drag that gray world you work in everywhere you go."

He touched one of his lapels. "This is a blue suit."

"Whoa. Cuttin' loose."

One dark eyebrow lifted. She was getting used to that, too.

"I'm here on business," he reminded her.

"You never heard of casual Friday?"

"It's my company, we don't *have* casual Friday."

"The fact that it's your company is the point. You could have casual Friday every day if you wanted to."

"I don't."

"Hence, the gray world," she said, walking again. "Life—conformity style."

Rick caught up with her in a couple of long strides. He was really tall—he towered over her. She liked the difference in their heights. She liked that he looked serious, but his eyes sparkled. Wow. Was that a glint of humor she saw there?

"You know, some people actually dress for success."

She shrugged. "I figure, success means you can dress however you want to."

"Ah, so I should be wearing jeans and a torn T-shirt."

"Nobody said anything about torn."

She took the five, freshly swept steps to the porch and stopped at the top. Turning around to face him, she had to look down, since he'd stopped at the bottom. "I don't remember you being such a stuffed shirt when you were a kid."

"I," he pointed out as he climbed the steps to stand eye level with her, "grew up."

She clutched her heart and grinned at him. "Cut to the bone."

"You're impossible, aren't you?"

"That's been said before."

"Not hard to believe."

For several moments they stood there looking at each other. Rick broke away while Eileen was still in a sexual trance. He bounded up the rest of the steps and crossed the wide porch.

He reached out, opened the door and held it for her to pass through in front of him. His gaze dropped over her before lifting to meet hers again. "Besides, I don't see you in jeans."

She smiled at him. "You will later."

"Can't wait."

Eileen stared up into his eyes and told herself to ignore the flash of heat that sizzled in those brown depths briefly before disappearing. She didn't need this complication.

Four

***

Their suite was bigger than the one he usually took when he stayed here. Of course, Rick thought, usually he didn't bring his secretary with him. Margo wouldn't have come along, preferring to be at home on the weekends with her husband. As for Eileen, he probably should never have pretended—to both of them—that he'd needed her on this trip.

Just the drive on the freeway had been torturous. His hormones were doing the kind of back flips they hadn't done since he'd hit puberty and had his first fantasy about...what the hell was her name? He shook his head. Didn't matter. And it would probably be a good idea to keep the word *fantasy* out of his mind, too.

God knows, he didn't need any encouragement.

He watched Eileen walk around the big living room, inspecting the whole place, from the books lining the bookshelves, to the hearth, already set and ready for a romantic fire. An overstuffed sofa in a pale flowered fabric crouched in front of the fireplace and two matching wing chairs sat on either side of it. Gleaming wood tables held vases of fresh flowers and dozens of scented candles dotted nearly every surface of the room.

"It's gorgeous."

He nodded. She certainly was. That black skirt of hers had been driving him nuts since she'd arrived at the office. She'd left her car in the parking lot at the office so they could drive down together. And during that long hour and a half, his gaze had slipped to her bare legs often. Her dark red shirt was plain, businesslike, and yet still managed to give his heart a kick start. Her hair, though, tempted him sorely. The long, loose waves draping around her shoulders made him want to spear his fingers through it. He'd had to keep a tight grip on the steering wheel, just to defeat the urge to reach out and see if her hair felt as soft as it looked.

"Shall I set up on that table?"

"Hmm?" He gave himself a mental shake and stared at her. "What?"

"The first meeting." She checked her silver wristwatch, then looked at him. "Your Mr. Harrington should be here in about twenty minutes."

"Yeah." Edward Harrington. Client. Business.

Good. Concentrate. "Sure. Uh, set up his files there and I'll order room service for when he gets here."

"I can take care of it."

"Fine." Rick picked up his suitcase. "Which bedroom do you want?"

"Doesn't matter," she said with a shrug. "Surprise me."

Something jumped inside him, but he buried it fast. The kind of surprise he'd like to show her had nothing to do with the choice of a bedroom, but what to do inside it. "You take the one on the right. I'll take this one."

He didn't wait for a response before escaping into the bedroom and shutting the door. Dropping his suitcase, he walked across the room to the tall bureau and stared at his reflection in the silvered mirror above it. Shoving both hands through his hair, he met his own gaze grimly. "Keep your mind on business, Hawkins. Anything else is just a world of trouble."

Lightning shimmered in the distance and thunder rolled across the sky to growl like a caged tiger in the living room of the suite. Eileen hugged herself and stepped through the French doors and out onto the narrow balcony. The wind slapped at her, lifting her hair and twisting it around her head in a wild tangle of curls. She reached up and scooped it back, then tipped her face into the wind, loving the feel of it rushing past her. The scent of coming rain surrounded her and she felt as if her skin was electrified by the building storm.

In the blustery weather, no one else was outside and they had the only balcony on this side of the house. It was private, secluded.

Behind her, lamplight glowed in a pale, golden haze over the table where Rick sat, still working over the last of Ed Harrington's file. She half turned to look at him and caught herself noticing how he ran his fingers through his hair. How his tie always crooked to the right when he was tired enough to loosen it. How his eyes shone in the lamplight. How his shoulders looked broader without the confines of his ever-present suit jacket.

Her blood pumped simply looking at him and she turned around, grateful that he was still immersed in his work. Just as well, she told herself, curling her fingers around the wrought-iron railing. They'd done fine all day, working side by side. She'd listened to him advising Ed about investments and his portfolios and even though she hadn't understood a word of it, she'd had to admit to being impressed.

But now that the work was finished for the day, her brain was free to think about other things. And not one of them had anything to do with his *brain*.

Lightning flashed, illuminating the edges of the clouds overhead and tracing white-hot, jagged fingers across the sky. Thunder boomed, closer this time.

"You're gonna get wet in a minute."

Her pulse quickened as Rick stepped out onto the

balcony beside her. "I love a storm," she said over the rumble of thunder. "We don't see many of them."

"Good thing. Had to shut the computer off because of the lightning."

Eileen smiled. "Poor worker bee. Had to stop."

"There's always the battery."

She nodded. "So why're you out here?"

He shifted his gaze from her to the storm-tossed sky. "Like you said, we don't see many of 'em." He leaned forward and braced his hands on the railing. "You were good today."

"Thanks." Nice compliment but she hadn't done all that much. Typing while they talked wasn't that tough.

He sighed and looked out over the garden below and the hills beyond the inn. "Edward's never talked that much. He's been a client for two years and I've never heard him talk about his late wife." Turning his head, he looked at her. "But you had him reminiscing inside a half hour."

"He thinks you're the greatest thing since sliced bread," she said, remembering how the older man had heaped praise on Rick. "He said you took his modest savings account and fixed it so that he doesn't have to worry—" she paused and smiled "—and that his grandkids will say great things about him because he left them so much money!"

Rick grinned and shook his head. "His grandkids are nuts about him. He takes them fishing every weekend."

"And he says that you've made lots of money for all of his friends," Eileen said, as if he hadn't spoken. "They buy him coffee every morning at the doughnut shop, just to thank him for referring you to them."

"That's nice to hear." His gaze drifted over her lazily.

"He says you're the smartest man he's ever met."

"He exaggerates."

"Maybe." But Eileen had to admit, she'd seen a whole new side of Rick today. Though to be fair, she'd been seeing him anew all week. The terrible boy he'd been was gone, and in his place was a thoughtful, intelligent man who was as careful with his clients' life savings as he would have been with his own grandmother's. Plus, he looked incredibly good when his tie was loose.

Whoops. Where did that come from?

"Ed's a sweetheart," she said quickly, jumping back to their conversation. "Sweet, sad and still lonely for the woman he loved most of his life."

"He enjoyed talking about her today."

She nodded. "All I did was listen. He was nice."

"Yeah," Rick agreed, staring into her eyes with a steadiness that made her shaky. "You're pretty nice yourself."

"Wow." She waved a hand at her face dramatically, as if to ease a nonexistent blush. "My little heart's fluttering."

"Uh-huh." A wry grin touched one corner of his

mouth. "Smells good out here," he said, and slid his hand on the railing until it brushed against hers.

Her skin heated, warmth rushing through her bloodstream. "It's the rain in the wind."

"Nope," he said, turning his head to look at her. "It's more like—" he leaned in closer to her, inhaled "—flowers."

Her breath caught when she stared into his eyes.

"It's you, Eileen." His gaze shifted, moving over her face, her throat, her breasts, and back up again.

"Rick…" She hadn't expected this. Hadn't expected him to say anything about the tension simmering between them. And now that he had, she wasn't sure what to do about it.

Her body, on the other hand, knew just what to do. Her heartbeat crashed in her ears, louder than the thunder booming out around them. Heat spiraled through her body, churning her insides, fogging her brain, liquefying her knees.

He drew back and turned his head to stare out into the night and the blustering storm. "Forget it," he muttered. "Shouldn't have said anything. Just let it go."

She should, Eileen told herself. If there was ever a moment to pay attention, to take an order, now was it. She should do just what he said and forget he'd ever opened this particular can of worms.

But she wouldn't.

Couldn't.

"Don't want to let it go," she admitted, and her

words were nearly swallowed by the next slam of thunder.

He snapped her a look and slowly straightened, reaching for her, drawing her up close. "We should, though."

"Right." She laid her hands on his forearms. "We don't even like each other."

"Yeah. You're a flake."

"And you're wound so tight, in a hundred years, you'll be a diamond."

"So," he said, "we forget the whole thing."

"That would be the reasonable thing to do," she said, and swept her hands up his arms to encircle his neck.

"I want you more than my next breath," he said tightly. "Screw reason."

His mouth came down on hers just as another, bigger, slash of lightning scraped jagged fingers across the sky. Brilliant light flashed before her closed eyelids and Eileen felt the sizzle in the air. As the following thunder boomed around them, it seemed to pale in comparison to the thudding of her own heart.

Rick lifted his head and stared down at her, his breath rushing from his lungs. Behind them, the room was dark, plunged into blackness.

"Power's out," he murmured.

"Not from where I'm standing," she said, meeting his gaze, her blood quickening on the hunger she read there.

A cold, strong wind whipped past them, wrapped

itself around their bodies like a frigid embrace, then dissolved in their combined heat. Lightning flashed, thunder rolled and desire, fed by the raging storm, clawed at them. Air rushed in and out of Eileen's lungs and still, she felt light-headed, as if a fog were settling over her brain, making thought impossible. But who needed to think when your blood was racing and your stomach was spinning and all points south were tingling in anticipation?

Rick must have felt the same because he took her mouth again. Hunger roared through her as he plundered her. His tongue parted her lips and swept into her warmth, tasting, exploring, plunging again and again into her depths. She welcomed him, her tongue meeting his in a tangled dance of need.

She arched forward, pressing herself into him, and moving, rubbing her aching nipples against his chest and torturing herself with the action. Her knees went weak and she tightened her grip on his shoulders to keep herself upright. His hands moved over her body, up and down her spine. He dragged her shirt free of the waistband of her skirt and skimmed his hands beneath it. Her skin tingled, firing with his touch until she felt as if every square inch of her body were bursting into flame.

He tore his mouth from hers and shifted lower, running his lips and tongue along her throat, tasting her pulse point at the base of her neck.

Eileen groaned and tipped her head back, inviting more, silently asking for more. And he gave. His lips and tongue teased her. His teeth nibbled at her skin, sending ripples of awareness and greed dancing through her. She clung to him, digging her fingers into his shoulders and, even while her brain sizzled with sensation, she was alert enough to notice that beneath his starched white shirt, his muscles had muscles.

"I can't get enough of the taste of you," he muttered, his breath dusting her skin as his words quickened her pulse.

He dropped his hands to the waistband of her skirt again and Eileen hung on as she heard and felt the zipper slide down. As soon as the black fabric was parted, he shoved it down over her hips. She felt the fabric slip along her legs and pool at her feet. Quickly, eagerly, she stepped free of the skirt and kicked it aside.

Cold, damp air caressed her bare skin, but she was too hot to care. Nothing mattered but the touch of his hands on her body. The feel of his mouth across her skin. And she needed more. Needed all of him. Now. She shifted her hold on him, her hands moving around to the front of his shirt. Quickly, deftly, her fingers undid the buttons on that white conservative business shirt and once she had the fabric parted, she scooped her hands across the white T-shirt beneath. Even through the warm cotton fabric, she felt the clearly defined muscles he hid so well.

He sucked in air through clenched teeth, then let her go long enough to pull off his dress shirt, then yank off the T-shirt.

"Wow," she murmured, her gaze dropping to the

broad expanse of his chest. His flesh was golden-brown, still tanned from summer, and deeply cut, with each muscle defined as if by an unseen sculptor. She ran the flat of her hands across his skin, twining her fingers through the dusting of brown curls and smiling when his breath hitched. "You're hiding an awful lot under those suits and ties."

He grinned wickedly. "You ain't seen nothin' yet."

Her stomach pitched and deep within her the flames burned hotter.

Rick reached for her, his fingers tearing at her shirt buttons. Hell, why'd they have to make buttons so damn small? Impatience drove him and he damn near gave in to the driving urge to just rip the blouse off her body. But then the last of the buttons slid free and he was pushing the shirt off her shoulders and looking down at the silky, dark red teddy she wore. Lace decorated the bodice, caressing the tops of her breasts. Her nipples, hard, erect, pushed against the fragile fabric and his mouth watered. He wanted to taste her. All of her. He wanted her beneath him, he wanted her over him. He just wanted her.

More than he'd ever wanted anything.

Rick lifted both hands to cup her breasts and she wilted into him, tipping her head back, shaking that glorious hair. She moaned, her mouth opening on the sound, her tongue sliding across her bottom lip in a not too subtle message.

Lightning crackled again and the resulting boom

of thunder clapped directly overhead, rattling the windowpanes and electrifying the air. The scent of coming rain filled him, but it could have poured on them and he still wouldn't have moved. Holding her here, in the open. In the darkness with the crash of nature all around them, felt…right. He wanted her here. On the balcony.

Now.

His thumbs and forefingers tweaked her nipples, tugging, pulling, sliding over the tips, pulling the fabric taut and using it to torture her gently. She twisted, moving into him, pressing her abdomen against his erection until he couldn't stand the wait any longer. Letting her go briefly, he ordered, "Stay here."

He stepped into the darkened hotel suite, but in moments, he was back. While the storm raged around them, he tore the rest of his clothes off, then reached for her again.

"Just a second," she whispered brokenly, and tugged the hem of her red lace teddy up and over her head, baring her breasts to him. In the electrified night, her skin glowed with a creamy translucence. Dark red lace panties were all she wore and he ached to get her out of those, too.

She stepped into his embrace, and Rick's arms came around her, holding her close, pressing her body along the length of his. Bodies brushed together. Soft to hard, rough to smooth. And with each touch, the storm between them grew stronger.

"Gotta have you," he murmured against her

mouth as he took her bottom lip, and then her top lip between his teeth, tasting, nibbling, claiming.

"Oh yeah," she said, swallowing hard as she took a tiny bite of his neck. "Now. Please, now."

"Now," he agreed, and with one quick turn of his wrist, snapped the flimsy elastic band of her panties. The red silk dropped from her skin and lay like a forgotten flag on the balcony's gleaming wood floor.

Lifting her easily, he sat her on the narrow metal railing and she yelped at the kiss of cold iron on her bare behind. One brief spurt of panic shot through her, remembering that they were on the second story. But his hands were strong and warm, holding her safely, tightly. Then he kissed her again, taking her mouth in a long, fast, hard plunge of desire. Panic receded and the heat between them fired and exploded.

Tearing her mouth from his, she fought for air as she held tightly to his shoulders. "Now, Rick," she urged as she parted her legs for him, "I want you inside me. *Now.*"

Her hands on his shoulders speared heat through his body and it was all Rick could do to one-handedly slide the condom he'd retrieved from the bedroom into place. Then, without another thought beyond easing the turmoil raging within him, he pushed himself inside her.

She gasped and tipped her head back, staring wide-eyed up at the stormy sky.

His hands clutched her waist in a firm grip, holding her safely. Holding her to him. In and out, he rocked within her, claiming her, taking her, giving her all he could give and taking the same from her. Her hot body surrounded him, holding him as tightly as he held her.

Above them, lightning flashed again and again. Thunder roared, crashing down on them, muffling the sounds they made as they came together in an urgency that mirrored the strength of the storm.

Bodies meshed, breaths met, mouths claimed, hands gripped.

Eileen felt him slide in and out of her body and felt the quickening rush of expectation building within her. He drove her, pushing them both higher, faster, until all she could see was the lightning reflected in his eyes. Dazzling flashes of light dancing across deep brown pools of emotion, sensation and she lost herself in it—in *him.*

She felt wicked. Wild. Wanton.

Surrounded by the storm, the cold, sharp wind, scented with rain, pushed at them, enveloping them. The metal railing beneath her was cold and narrow, but Rick's hold on her made her feel safe enough to enjoy the thrill of the moment. To concentrate on nothing more than the hard, solid strength of him driving into her body.

Eileen lifted her legs and wrapped them around his waist as her climax neared. She moved into him, rocking as much as she dared, taking as much of him as he gave, offering herself and pulling him closer, deeper, within her.

The rain started.

Icy pellets of water sluiced over them in a rush.

As if the sky had reached the point of no return and hadn't been able to hold back any longer.

Eileen knew the feeling.

With rain cascading over them, she shook her wet hair back from her face and fought for breath. Her mind splintered. Her body exploded.

"Rick...Rick..." Her fingers flexed on his shoulders, her nails digging into his flesh, holding on, squeezing as he pushed her up that last, sweet climb to release. She looked into his eyes and watched him as he kissed her. His tongue swept across her lips, her teeth, moving inside, taking her breath and giving her his. She felt it all. Felt the magic build. Felt the sudden sway of her body tipping into oblivion, and then she groaned and rode the wave of completion, locked within his grasp, his mouth muffling her cries.

And before her body had stopped trembling, he plunged deep within her and stiffened, reaching his own release in time to join her on the slow slide down from heaven.

Five

————

His body still quivering with reaction, Rick lifted her off the railing, and keeping his body locked tight within hers, carried her inside, out of the rain.

She wrapped her arms around him and kept her legs twisted about his waist like a vise. Burying her face in the curve of his neck, she shuddered, then whispered, "Okay, *that* was impressive."

He chuckled, and holding her close, made his way carefully across the darkened living room to his bedroom. "And that was wet. I do my best work when I'm dry."

She lifted her head to look at him in the dim light. "Well heck," she said, "hand me a towel."

He gave her behind a sharp pat. "That's the plan."

"Love a man with a plan," Eileen said, keeping her gaze fixed on his as he stepped through the doorway and into his room.

Rocking her hips, she moved on him and he sucked in air through clenched teeth. Slapping one arm across her behind, he held her still. "You're killing me," he admitted.

"Oh," she said, shaking her head, letting water droplets fly, "not yet."

One corner of his mouth lifted as he eased down onto the soft mattress, his body still deep within hers. "Got your own plans, have you?"

"I'm making it up as I go along," she said, reaching to cup his face between her palms.

"You're doin' fine," he assured her. "Don't stop now."

"Don't worry about that." Now that they'd started, giving in to the tension that had rippled between them all week, Eileen didn't want to stop. She wanted more of him. She wanted to feel that building excitement within again. She wanted to experience the crashing explosion of desire and the throbbing pulse of satisfaction.

She hadn't expected this.

Hadn't planned on it.

But she was smart enough to enjoy it once it had happened.

The old quilt beneath her felt warm and soft. Cotton brushed her skin and wrapped up around her like a cocoon. She felt surrounded by warmth even though her skin had been chilled by the rain, now beating down on the roof like tiny fists in a fury. Occasional flashes of lightning were the only illumination in the room, but it was enough to see Rick's face, read his features, and know that he was feeling the same things she was.

He moved within her, hard again and she arched into him like a lazy cat waiting to be stroked. Tipping her head back into the mattress, she unwound her legs from his hips and planted both feet on the bed. Then rocking her hips against his, she opened wider for him, taking him as deeply as she could and wishing she could take him completely inside her. He was so big, so hard, she felt as though he was touching the base of her heart when he plunged inside her.

"More," she demanded, dragging her nails along his back, down his spine.

"More," he agreed and suddenly flipped over, taking her with him, until she straddled him and he lay flat on his back.

Rick watched her in the half-light and wished he'd taken the time to light some of the candles that were sprinkled around the room. Apparently there were lots of power outages around here. And a few lit candles would have been enough to let him completely enjoy the sight of Eileen atop him.

With her legs on either side of him, she braced her palms on his chest and fingered his flat nipples, stroking, caressing. She moved on him, rocking her hips and bucking, arching her back as though she were riding a half-wild horse in a rodeo.

Her skin still damp with rain, cold drops of water dripping from the ends of her hair to splatter against his body, she looked fierce and tender and free. Her head fell back and her eyes closed as she moved on him, taking him deep within her and grinding her hips against him. She drove him higher, higher than he'd expected. Higher than he'd thought possible. And the flashing need erupting inside him nearly strangled him.

He reached up, covering her breasts with his hands, his fingers and thumbs squeezing her hardened nipples. She pushed herself into his touch and he smiled, before dropping one hand to the spot where their bodies met. He fingered her center, toying with that small nubbin of flesh that held her secrets, cradled her need.

"Rick!" She groaned his name and moved harder on him, swaying, moving with a rhythm that rocked him to his bones.

"Feel it," he ordered, watching her face, seeing the pleasure streaking across her features.

"Too much," she murmured, shaking her head, biting her bottom lip.

"Never enough," he told her, and kept stroking her center as she moved on him, rocking, swaying, taking.

She gasped as her body tightened on his. The first tremors took her and she moved quickly, fiercely, heightening her own pleasure while demanding his.

"Never enough," she echoed as he erupted inside

her, then cradled her gently as they took the fall together.

Minutes, hours...heck, it could have been *days* later, for all Eileen knew—or cared—she collapsed beside him in a boneless heap. She licked her lips and tried to fight off the buzzing in her head long enough to say, "That was... amazing."

"In a word," he said, his voice nearly lost in the crash and boom of thunder.

"You know..." Eileen took a long, unsteady breath and blew it out again before continuing. "For a guy who looks like Mr. Uptight and Closed Off, you do some great work."

"You're not so bad yourself," he said.

She smiled in the darkness, then felt that smile slowly fade away as reality came crashing down on her. "We're gonna be sorry we did this, aren't we?"

"Probably."

"That's what I thought." Eileen studied the play of slashes of light across the beamed ceiling and listened to Rick's heavy breathing in the quiet. Her thoughts raced across her mind in such a blur of speed she couldn't really nail one down long enough to examine it. And that was, no doubt, for the best. Considering that if she really stopped to think about what she'd just done with Rick, she'd probably smack herself in the forehead.

"I want you to know," she said, "I'm not looking for a relationship."

"Me neither."

"That's good, then."

"Yeah. Good."

"Still, this is going to complicate things, isn't it?" she asked.

"You mean, am I going to look at you sitting at your desk and picture you here?" he asked. "Oh yeah."

"It's not going to be easy for me either, you know." She couldn't even imagine being in the office with him and *not* thinking about those wild moments out on the balcony. Stupid, Eileen. Really stupid. She shouldn't have done this. Shouldn't have given in to her hormones like some vapid teenager who didn't know better.

She should have remembered that men were trouble and her track record was less than stellar.

"Which is why we shouldn't have."

"True." Eileen glanced at him, and noted that he, too, was staring up into the darkness. She wondered what he was really thinking. If he was wondering how to make a graceful exit from the bed. If he'd just fire her right now and avoid the whole embarrassing after-sex scene. "I'm only in your life —your world, temporarily. Two weeks. That's it."

"Should have been simple," he said.

"Not anymore."

"Nope."

She sighed and turned onto her side. Heat from his body reached out for her and she couldn't resist touching him again. Sliding one hand up his chest, she murmured, "Just think, our grandmothers got us into this."

He chuckled, caught her hand and threaded his fingers through hers. "I don't think this is what they had in mind."

"Hardly."

"Look," Rick said, his voice gaining strength, his fingers tightening on her hand. "What happened, happened. We're adults. It shouldn't be any big thing to deal with. It was just sex."

"Amazing sex."

"That goes without saying."

"It'd be nice to hear, though."

He looked at her. "Amazing sex."

"Thank you."

"No," he countered, "thank *you*."

"Trust me," she said, a reluctant smile curving her mouth. "My pleasure."

"Yeah, I know."

"No ego problems here."

He rolled over, pushing her onto her back and bracing himself up one elbow so that he could look down at her. "It's one night. One night out of a lifetime. Neither one of us is looking for—or expects—roses and cherubs. We enjoy each other, then go back to business as usual tomorrow."

Eileen looked up at him, studying his eyes, his face, the curve of his mouth. She wanted to kiss him again. To taste him. To feel his tongue sweeping against hers. Hunger arced inside her again, fresh, greedy. She'd never felt like this before.

She'd been with a man before, of course. Her fiancé and then Joshua. But those experiences were nothing compared to what was going on inside her at the moment. She'd never felt the compulsion for more as she had tonight.

Even though she'd just been with Rick, she wanted him again. Now. Inside her. She wanted to feel his body moving within hers. Wanted to feel a part of him. Wanted to be locked within his embrace—and that was new.

A part of her wanted to explore these new sensations. And another, more wary part of her wanted to back off now, while she could still think logically. There was no future with Rick. He was just like every other man she'd ever come across. He wanted her to help him out at work. He wanted her in his bed. But, like every other male in her life, he didn't want *her*. This wasn't a relationship. This was simply two people who felt a...connection. Was that enough reason to enjoy each other? And could they keep it that simple?

"Can we do that, do you think?"

"I can," Rick said, smoothing his fingertips across her cheek, pushing her hair back behind her ear. Looking at her now made him want her again. And yet he knew he would be able to say goodbye. Because he *had* to. He wouldn't let her get close. Couldn't let her in. He'd taken one chance and got smacked for his trouble. He wouldn't be doing that again.

Rick had learned years ago that life was easier if

lived alone. Sex was one thing. Love—a relationship—was something else. Something he wasn't interested in. "So the question is," he asked, "can you?"

She shivered at his touch, the tiny bursts of heat transferring from his fingers to her skin. Could she forget what happened tonight in tomorrow's light of day? She wasn't sure. Could she give up the chance to feel more of what she already had? No way. So there was really only one answer to his question.

"Yes, I can."

"Good," he said, and pulled away from her.

"I say yes and you leave?"

He pushed off the bed and turned back to look at her again, a smile tipping one corner of his mouth. Her heart jumped in response.

"Just going to light a few of these candles," he said. "This time I want to see you."

"Oh, boy."

She looked beautiful by candlelight.

Tiny flames flickered around the room, tracing halos of golden light against the flowered wallpaper. Beyond the windows, the storm still raged, rain pelting at the glass, lightning and thunder growling and snapping, like ferocious beasts demanding entry. The four-poster bed looked wide and soft and compelling, as Eileen lay across the clean white sheets, her bare body a temptation no man could resist.

And Rick had no desire to resist her.

He couldn't remember ever feeling this hunger before. The sizzle and snap of heat that burst into life every time he touched her made him yearn to feel it again. Watching the candlelight play on her smooth, pale skin made his palms itch to touch her again.

Eileen was unlike any woman he'd ever known.

Hell, everything about her was different.

Unique.

Her attitude, her laugh, her scent. She smelled of roses and sunlight—a compelling mixture to a man too used to burying himself under mountains of work, shut away in corporate towers. She laughed at his work ethic. Teased him about taking himself too seriously and fought him when he gave orders. And he was enjoying himself far too much.

Which should have worried him—but he was too hungry for the taste of her to think about it now.

He crossed the room to her, his skin tingling in anticipation of the brush of her body against his.

She went up on both elbows, cocked her head to one side and smiled. "You know, something just occurred to me."

The pale light in the room danced on the ends of her still damp hair and glistened in the water drops like diamonds. That stray thought brought him up short. Hell, he'd never been particularly poetic before. "Yeah? What's that?"

She drew one leg up, sliding the sole of her foot up the length of her other leg in a long, slow caress that caught his gaze and stole his breath.

"Do you always go armed with condoms when you travel with your secretary?"

He stopped at the edge of the bed and dropped one hand to her calf, smiling when her eyes closed at his touch. His fingers drifted along her skin with a feather-light caress. "Nope. Remember when we stopped for gas?"

"Uh-huh," she murmured as his hand slid higher, higher, past her knee, up along her thigh.

Rick smiled, remembering the impulse that had told him to buy a couple of the dusty packages of condoms he'd found on a back shelf. "Stop-and-shop gas stations carry a lot of items these days."

She dropped backward onto the mattress and arched her hips as his fingers brushed the juncture of her thighs. She sucked in a gulp of air and released it from her lungs slowly. "Thank heaven, you're a careful shopper."

He watched her through narrowed eyes. Flickering light played across her features as she practically vibrated under his touch. "One of my many gifts."

"What's another?" She lifted her hips into his hand, her breath hitching as his fingertips stroked her center.

"You're about to find out." Rick's heartbeat pounded in his ears. Blood rushed through his veins, creating a heat that made him feel as though he were standing in the center of a roaring fire. His breathing strangled, he gave into the urges riding him and grabbed her legs. Pulling her quickly around, he turned her abruptly on the mattress and yanked her toward him.

"Hey!" She grabbed at the sheets beneath her as if holding on.

"Shut up, Ryan."

"Excuse me?" She lifted her head to stare at him.

Tugging her to the edge of the bed, he spread her legs with a gentle touch, then sank to his knees in front of her. "I said shut up."

"What the he—" She stared down at him. "Rick…"

He looked at her and his breath stopped. Candlelight danced in her eyes and brushed her skin with a soft golden haze. She looked beautiful and wild and lush enough to steal a man's soul.

If he let her.

Rick wouldn't.

He just had to have her.

"Trust me," he whispered, his voice a hush, lost in the fury of the storm beyond the cozy, softly lit room.

Lifting first one of her legs and then the other, Rick laid them across his shoulders, then scooped his hands under her bottom. Her body trembled and she arched her hips, squirming as if trying to free herself. But she wasn't trying hard.

"Rick, you don't have to—" She reached one hand out to him.

"Like I said—shut up, Ryan." He locked his gaze with hers as he took her. His mouth covered her center. Her eyes went wide, her mouth dropped open and air rushed from her lungs in a whoosh.

She watched him take her, and feeling her gaze

on him fed his own hunger. He licked her soft flesh and she whimpered, threading her fingers through his hair and holding him to her as if afraid he'd stop. She needn't have worried. He couldn't stop. The feel of her body melting beneath his touch inflamed him. Her sighs filled him. He tasted her, dipping his tongue within her tender flesh, sending her higher than she'd ever been before.

One hand kneaded her bottom while he swept the other around to dip first one finger, and then two, into her depths. She shuddered, lifting herself into his mouth.

''Rick, that…feels…so…*good.* Don't stop. Don't ever stop.''

Her broken voice, her breathy words, carried on the next clap of thunder, and he instinctively gave her more, pushing her farther, faster.

Eileen moved with him, rocking her hips, reaching for the wonder she knew was waiting for her. She watched him, unable to tear her gaze from the sight of him taking her so intimately. His gaze burned into hers. Candlelight flickered over his features and he looked dark, dangerous and too damn good.

He lifted her bottom off the bed and she was dangling in his grasp, his mouth the only stable point in her world. His hot breath dusted her most intimate flesh and his fingers and tongue worked her body into a frenzy of sensation that pooled in her center and spiraled throughout her insides. Her heartbeat drummed in her ears. Her breath staggered. She couldn't hold out much longer. Couldn't make it last, despite wanting his mouth on her forever. The end was crashing down on her and she rushed to meet it.

She cupped the back of his head, holding him to her as she cried out his name. He kept kissing her until the last of the tremors subsided and, when she thought she might shatter, he eased her back into the middle of the bed.

Her vision blurred as she looked up at him, kneeling between her legs. "You're just full of surprises, aren't you?"

"I try."

"Well, you're doin' fine," she assured him, and told herself that it didn't matter if her heartbeat was somewhere around three hundred. If she died of a heart attack right now, she'd meet death with a satisfied smile on her face.

"Glad to hear it." He grinned and leaned over to snag another condom from the bedside table. As he tore the foil packet open, he looked back at her. New desire shimmered in his eyes, sending a wicked spiral of want and need spinning through her. Surprise and pleasure shifted inside her, opening her to more sensations, making her wonder where this was all leading. Making her stop and think. Which she didn't want to do at the moment.

Thankfully, Rick splintered her thoughts and sent them packing when he asked with a wink, "Ready to go again?"

Six

In the candlelight, his skin gleamed like polished oak. Every well-defined muscle stood out in sharp relief and all Eileen could think of was that she wanted to trace every inch of his body with her fingers. Her lips. She wanted him as she'd never wanted anyone before. She couldn't seem to get enough of him. And that thought shimmered briefly in her mind before she set it aside to explore later.

There would be plenty of time for thinking once the sun came up and their one-night bargain ended. For now… there was Rick. Nothing else.

"Sleep," she said, "is vastly overrated."

"Is that right?"

"Oh yeah," she said, and squirmed slightly on the bed, scooting closer to him, feeling the brush of his hardened body against her core. "It's a known fact. You don't need more than twenty minutes sleep a night to function at your best."

"That's a relief," he said, pulling the condom from the packet.

"Wait," she said. "Let me." She snatched the condom from his grasp. Half sitting up, she covered the tip of him with the pale latex, then slowly, sinuously, rolled it down along his length.

He sucked in air with a hiss.

Her fingers folded around him and squeezed gently.

His eyes closed and a muscle in his jaw twitched.

She touched him, sliding her fingers up and down the hard, solid length of him, then stopped to boldly cup him. His eyes opened and the candlelight reflected in those dark depths made him look dangerous again as he pulled her hand away.

"That's it," he muttered, and leaned over her. He grasped both of her wrists in one tight fist, holding her hands against the bed, high over her head. She writhed and twisted beneath him on the bed, moving into him, lifting her hips, inviting him in.

Rick surrendered to the fury pulsing within. Desire scratched at him. Need howled inside him. Hunger raged in him. And when he pushed himself into her body, it all escalated. His heartbeat raced, his blood pumped and his breath staggered in and out of his lungs. All he could hear was her sighs. All he could feel was her breath as he lowered himself to kiss her. She nibbled at his mouth and planted her feet on the mattress to rock her body against his.

She was all.

She was everything.

And for tonight, she was *his*.

Releasing his grip on her wrists, he groaned when she dragged her nails along his back. Then she pulled his head to her breasts and he pleased her, suckling, drawing, pulling at her nipples, first one, then the other. The scent of her drove him wild, the taste of her created hungers he'd never known before.

They moved together, two shadows in the candle-light. And while the storm raged beyond the windows, two souls found something neither of them had been looking for.

Dawn arrived sooner than they would have wanted.

"Storm's over," Eileen said, knowing Rick was lying beside her, wide-awake.

"Yeah, looks like."

Rain dripped from the eaves, sounding like a clock, ticking away the last seconds of an incredible night. The first brush of daylight softened the room, obliterating the light from what was left of the candles. Most of them had guttered out in their own wax hours ago. The last few were unnecessary now.

Eileen winced and shifted position, tugging the edge of the quilt up over her breasts. Though why she was bothering with modesty at this late date was beyond her. There wasn't one square inch of her body that Rick hadn't seen, tasted or explored.

She slapped one hand across her eyes and tried not to think too much about everything they'd done together in the dark.

"Regrets?" he asked, his voice a low rumble close to her ear.

She thought about that for a long minute. Did she regret any of it? Could she? He'd made her feel things she'd merely read about. He'd made her body sing. No. She didn't regret it. She was only sorry their agreement had been for one night only. Though it was probably safest that way. She wasn't going to get involved here and she knew darn well that if she kept sleeping with him, her heart *would* make the leap whether she wanted it to or not. So in the spirit of self-preservation, she'd stick to the bargain despite the clamoring of her hormones. "No. No regrets."

"You had to think about it, though," he teased her.

Turning her head on the pillow, she looked at him. In the early morning light, he looked just as good as he did in candlelight. "What about you?"

He slid one hand up her body, across her rib cage to cup one of her breasts.

She sucked in a gulp of air.

"No regrets," he said, and leaned in close enough to kiss her. Then he pulled away, rolling onto his back to stare up at the ceiling.

"So," Eileen said, feeling the loss of his hand on her body, "now we get up, get showered and move on."

"Right," he said.

Boy, that had sounded like a good idea the night before. Now though…she sat up and swung her legs off the edge of the bed, before she could do something really dumb like suggest that they pretend it wasn't morning yet. "Night's over, so we're finished."

"Exactly. Back to business."

"Right," she said. She was achy all over. Muscles she hadn't used in ages were shrieking at her. And still, it was all Eileen could do to keep from turning back around and jumping on to him. She stood up and walked across the room toward the door, snatching up the complimentary plush white robe on the bench at the end of the bed. Slipping into its warmth, she belted it at the waist and paused in the doorway to look back at him. "I'll go over to my room, hop in the shower and then meet you in the living room for breakfast in an hour or so?"

He went up on one elbow, his dark brown hair falling across his forehead to give him a rakish air he wouldn't have once he was back in one of his blasted suits. Her palms itched to smooth across his chest again. To feel his heart beating beneath her touch. She curled her fingers into fists and shoved her hands into the robe's pockets.

"An hour," he said tightly, and watched her go.

* * *

Standing under the pulsating jets of hot water, Eileen struggled to clear her mind. To push the night's memories into a dark corner, where they couldn't sneak out to taunt her. But it was no use.

Hot, needlelike punches of water beat on her body in staccato bursts from the shower massage and reminded her of his hands on her. Of his mouth. Of his touch. Of the fires he could stoke with a look.

And she ached for him.

At the slide of the curtain rings on the metal pole, she turned in time to see him step naked into the shower behind her. "Rick—"

He grabbed her and pulled her close, sliding her water-slick body along his. "Sun's not all the way up yet. Night's not over."

She stared up at his taut features, swallowed hard and said, "Works for me."

Turning her around, Rick pressed her back up against the shower wall and lifted her off her feet. Steam from the shower rose up like a soft fog, enveloping them in a small, private world. Water pounded on his back like a heartbeat. She wrapped her legs around his waist and he entered her with one quick lunge that stole his breath. He'd tried to stay away. But hearing the water, knowing she was naked and wet and warm, was simply too much of a temptation to ignore.

Now he moved within her, racing toward the ecstasy that had become familiar during the long night. Burying his face in the curve of her throat, he gave himself to her and took all she had to give.

* * *

An hour later, they were in her bed, having breakfast. Wrapped in the thick terry robes, they shared strawberries, Belgian waffles and hot coffee.

"When does your first client get here?" Eileen asked, biting into a fresh ripe strawberry direct from the inn's greenhouse.

Rick checked the bedside clock. "About an hour."

She nodded. "Probably a good thing, huh?"

He looked at her and all he could think was that he wanted to taste her strawberry-stained mouth. His body stirred and even he was amazed. He should be exhausted, yet he felt more awake, more alive than he ever had before. She was like a jolt of pure electricity. She kept his body humming and his blood pumping and he hadn't had nearly enough of her yet. "Yeah," he murmured. "A good thing." Pouring more coffee into both their mugs, he said, "There are three meetings today and one tomorrow morning."

"Okay."

"If you want to, later we can go out. There's an Indian casino near here. We can catch a show."

"Sounds good."

Rick winced at the stiffness in her voice. Hell, in *his* voice. "Look, we don't have to be this polite and formal with each other," he said, hating the distance springing up between them, even though he knew it was for the best. No point in dragging this on, right? Not when he knew damn well he'd be saying goodbye to her in another week. And he *would* say goodbye.

That's what he did.

He didn't stick around and give women the chance to leave him. Not again. Not ever again. "We had a good time," he said. "Now it's over."

"Right," she said, and relaxed back against the headboard. "We're adults—neither one of us is committed to someone else. No reason we can't walk away. We can do this."

He smiled at her. "Just as well we're not going to be having another night like last one."

"Why?" She cradled her coffee cup between her palms.

Rick grinned and took a sip of the hot, rich brew. "When Mrs. Hammond brought the breakfast tray up here, she asked me if I'd heard anything unusual during the night."

Eileen's eyes went wide. "Unusual?"

"Uh-huh. Seems that just before the rain started, she heard a loud yelp."

She clapped one hand across her mouth. "Oh, God."

He chuckled and shook his head. "Don't worry. She thought a coyote had gotten hold of some small animal."

"A *coyote?*"

"Yeah. Apparently, you hit just the right note to sound like a dying rabbit."

She bounced a pillow off his head.

* * *

"Okay, this no more sex thing just isn't working out."

"Yeah, I noticed." Rick rolled to one side of her and lay on his back, struggling to catch his breath.

Lying naked on the braided rug in front of the fireplace, Eileen winced and reached beneath her. She pulled a ballpoint pen out from under her bottom. "That's what that was."

"Huh?"

"The pen your last client lost?" she asked, holding it up. "I found it."

Rick chuckled, then shook his head. "What the hell are we doing, Eyeball?"

"Beats me, Hawkins." Holding the stupid pen, she let her hand drop, falling across her abdomen. "But if we don't figure it out soon, we're gonna end up killing each other."

The last client had only left the inn an hour ago and already, Eileen and Rick were naked and exhausted. Sexual heat still shimmered in the air and Eileen felt the first stirrings of need building within her again. Much more of this and they'd be too weak to drive home.

They'd made it through the long day, though the tension between them had been thick enough to chew on. Eileen had taken notes, typed them up and helped Rick draw up the paperwork for two of his clients to diversify their stock holdings. She'd made small talk and tried to avoid meeting Rick's gaze. She'd felt him watching her as his clients came and went. She'd smiled and visited with the older men who, each in turn, told her what a great catch Rick Hawkins would be. How smart he was. How rich.

Of course, when the talk had turned in that direction, Eileen had actually *seen* shutters drop across his eyes. As if he was distancing himself from the conversation, even though he had to know the men had only been teasing. She'd had the urge to tell him that he was safe. She wasn't interested in a "great catch" or any other kind of catch. But in front of his clients, that hadn't seemed appropriate— and once she and Rick were alone…well, the subject hadn't come up.

"Well," he said finally, "our one-night bargain is shot."

"Pretty much," she agreed.

"Do we make a new one-night agreement?"

"That would technically be a *two*-night bargain."

"Fine. Two nights. Whatever."

She turned her head to look at him. "Whoa. Lack of sleep making somebody cranky?"

"No." He met her gaze. "It's not sleep I'm craving."

Eileen's stomach flip-flopped, then did a slow whirl. "Me neither, big boy," she admitted, then added, "but before this turns into the Lost Weekend, we'd better have some ground rules."

He rolled onto his side and propped his head on his hand. "Rules are good."

Eileen chuckled. Now there was a statement on his personality. "Figured you'd say that."

She too went onto her side and lay facing him. Flames danced in the hearth behind him, sending ripples of light around the room and gilding the ends of his hair until he looked almost as if he were wearing a halo.

Rick Hawkins? A halo?

Okay, rules were definitely in order!

Idly he reached out one hand to stroke her breast. Eileen hissed in a breath and let it out again. "First," she said, a little more loudly than she'd planned, "no strings."

"Agreed," he said, his now-narrowed gaze focused on hers. "I'm not looking for anything permanent."

"Ditto." She caught a flicker of surprise in his eyes and addressed it. "What? You think every woman you meet is trying to lure you into a bear trap?"

One dark eyebrow lifted, managing to convey a world of comments.

"You can relax on that score, Mr. Wonderful," she assured him. "You're completely safe."

"No strings means what, exactly?" he prompted, ignoring her last statement.

"I guess it means we enjoy what we have while we have it," Eileen said, and gulped when his talented fingers tweaked her nipple. Closing her eyes briefly, she opened them again and stared directly into his. "When one of us has had enough, it's over. Deal?"

"Deal."

"Shouldn't we shake hands on it?"

A corner of his mouth tipped up. "Oh, we can do better than that."

The rest of the weekend was a blur.

A good blur, but a blur.

On Sunday afternoon, Eileen walked into her house, left her small, rolling suitcase in the foyer, then dropped onto the worn overstuffed sofa. Its soft down-filled cushions came up around her like a warm hug. Propping her feet up on the mission-style coffee table, she scraped both hands across her face and tried to figure out how she'd work a temporary affair into her world.

God, she hadn't planned on this. Who would have guessed that Rick Hawkins would be the man who could light up her insides like a Christmas tree? And who would have thought that a two-week favor to her grandmother would turn into…she dropped her hands onto her lap. Turn into what? What exactly had happened? One red-hot weekend?

Because if that's all it turned out to be, a part of her would be sorry. She didn't really want to get involved with anybody, but on the other hand, it had been a long time since she'd been with a man. A long time since she'd felt…close, to anyone. And damn it, she'd enjoyed it. Not just the sex, she thought, though she had to admit, Rick had a real gift in that area, but it was more than that. It was laughing with him. Talking to him. It was midnight meals and napping in front of the fire. It was long walks on windswept hills and hearing him try to explain the securities market.

It was a lot of things she hadn't expected.

She hadn't felt anything remotely like this since just before she'd broken off her engagement to Robert Bates. Frowning, Eileen grabbed one of the green plaid throw pillows and hugged it to her chest. He'd been her college boyfriend. Pre-med when she met him, they'd made plans for the future. Eileen had planned their wedding, their marriage and even how many kids they'd have—three—two boys and a girl. And then at graduation, Robert had suggested they not get married right away. Instead, he wanted her to go to work. They could live together, he'd said, and she could support him while he finished med school. *Then,* if the time was right, they'd get married.

Sighing, Eileen let her head fall back against the cushions. "But the time was never going to be right," she muttered, remembering the look of surprise on Robert's face when she came home early from work one night. Of course, the girl he was on top of was pretty surprised, too—but it was Robert's expression that had stayed with her. Not hurt, not defeated or even guilty. Just angry. Angry at *her* for not being at work, like the good little cash cow he'd expected her to be.

She'd grabbed up as many of her clothes as she could and walked out, leaving Robert and his floozy right where she'd found them. That was the last time she'd trusted her heart to anybody. And she'd vowed then that she wouldn't do it again.

"But this is different," she argued to the empty room. "It's not my heart involved here...just my hormones."

Her own words echoed in the quiet and even *she* didn't quite believe them. But she would. All she had to do was keep reminding herself that this whole situation was temporary.

"Yeah," she said, pushing up from the couch. "That'll work."

Seven

———

"**Y**our grandma called," Eileen said as she poked her head into Rick's office Monday morning.

He looked up. "What line is she on?"

"No, *called*," she repeated. "Past tense." Leaning against the doorjamb, she folded her arms over her chest and looked at him. "She said to tell you she didn't have time to talk. She booked a last-minute Fall Foliage train trip and she still had to shop for clothes."

Rick smiled to himself. His grandmother would never change. She treated life like an adventure. She never bothered to plan something out. She thought there was no fun in anything if it wasn't spontaneous. Hence, her trip to watch the space shuttle launch. And apparently, fall leaves. "When's she coming back?"

Eileen laughed shortly. "She wasn't sure. But she did say she tried to get my gran to join her."

"Is she?"

"No." She straightened up and walked across his office to stand in front of his desk. "When Gran takes a trip, she likes to go to the auto club and stock up on maps months in advance. Half the fun, she says, is planning her route."

"Your grandmother plans, and mine's a free spirit," he murmured, leaning back in his chair to study her. "Ever think we were switched at birth?"

"Possibility. I used to plan things. I gave it up."

"How'd you sleep?" he asked, his voice dropping a notch or two, until the sound of it scraped along her spine and sent a shiver of expectation rattling through her.

"Fine. You?"

"Great."

"Good."

"Good," he said, his gaze locked on hers and burning with unspoken words. "I missed—"

She held her breath.

"—breakfast in bed," he finished.

"Me too."

"With you, I mean," Rick said, standing up and moving around the edge of his desk. "I missed a lot of things. Missed hearing you breathing in the dark."

"Rick…"

"I missed reaching for you and finding you there, hot and ready."

"Yeah well," Eileen admitted after inhaling sharply, "I kind of missed being reached for."

"So what're we gonna do?"

"I guess we're gonna keep this going for a while, huh?"

"Is that what you want?" he asked.

"Depends. Is it what you want?"

He took her hand and yanked her close enough that she could feel his hard strength pressing into her abdomen. "You tell me."

"Okeydoke, then." Her body burst into flames. She knew because her mouth was suddenly dry. "After work. My place?"

"After work," he repeated, and reluctantly released her. "But for now," he said as he walked back to his desk chair, "I need to see the Baker files."

"You bet," she said, and turned around, headed back to the outer office. She felt him watching her with every step.

Two hours later, Rick was closeted with a client and Eileen's phone was ringing.

"Hawkins Financial."

"Hello, honey!"

Eileen smiled into the phone. "Hi, Gran."

"How's it going?"

She opened her mouth, then closed it again, pausing to think. Hmm. How to describe what was going on around here. "It's going…fine." Safe, boring and as far from the truth as she could get. But what else was she going to tell her grandma? That Rick was the best sex she'd ever had?

Good God.

Right after recovering from her heart attack, Gran would drag Eileen to St. Steven's and stretch her out prostrate on the altar. Nope. Sometimes a comfortable lie was better than the truth.

"Good. I knew everything would work out as soon as you were able to let go of the whole 'Rick was mean to me' issue from your childhood."

"Issue?" Eileen pulled the phone from her ear and stared at it for a moment through thoughtful, narrowed eyes. Then she snapped it back and asked, "Have you been watching that talk show again?"

"Dr. Mike is a very smart man," Gran said.

"Oh," she said dryly, "I'll bet." Gran's favorite TV psychologist had an answer for everything from hair loss to potty training and wasn't the least bit shy about sharing them. And women like her grandmother ate it up.

"He's simply trying to help people face and confront their fears." A long pause. "You might think about watching him sometime, dear."

Eileen sighed and pulled her hands back from the keyboard. Giving the closed door to Rick's office a quick look, she said, "I don't have any fears to confront, Gran. But thanks for thinking of me."

"Commitment-phobic people always claim that."

"What?" Her eyes bugged out and Eileen

slapped one hand over them to prevent another contact lens search.

"Dr. Mike says that people who are afraid to get hurt should just jump in and take the risk anyway. It's healthy."

"Dr. Mike can kiss my—"

"Eileen Ryan!"

"Gran." Instantly apologetic, Eileen remembered where she was and lowered her voice. "I'm sorry. But seriously, stop trying to cure me by watching television. *And,* I don't need a cure. There's nothing wrong with me, anyway."

"Nothing a husband and kids wouldn't fix," her grandmother argued.

Eileen's chin hit her chest. Gran had been singing the same song for years. "Not everyone is going to live happily ever after, you know? Not everyone wants to."

"Yes, but *you* do. I know you're lonely, Eileen. Do you think I don't notice how you watch Bridie and her family? Do you think I don't see that sheen of tears in your eyes when you hold the baby?"

Eileen huffed out a sigh. Fine. So she felt a little sorry for herself sometimes. Who didn't? Did that make her a potential customer for Dr. Mike? No, she didn't think so. What it made her was human. Sure she envied Bridie's happiness a little. But Eileen was happy, too. Her life was just the way she wanted it.

And the phrase, *methinks you protest too much,*

floated through her mind before she had a chance to cut it off at the pass.

"Look, Gran," she said quickly, "I've gotta go. Rick needs something." A small lie, she plea-bargained with the gods as they no doubt made a little black mark on her soul. Lying to sweet old ladies didn't go down real well in the world of Karma.

"Fine, fine, I don't want to keep you," Gran said in the tone that clearly said she wasn't ready to hang up yet.

"I'll call you later."

"Come for dinner."

"I—*can't*," she said, remembering that she'd be busy after work. "But I'll call. Promise."

"All right, but I really think you should—"

"Gotta go, Gran. Seriously." Eileen bent over her desk, still talking while she lowered the receiver toward its base. "Honest. Gotta go." Her grandmother was still talking. "Bye."

Then she hung up, knowing that she'd be paying for that one later.

Sitting back in her chair, Eileen thought about everything Gran had said. Lonely? Sure, she was lonely sometimes. Wasn't everyone? But on the whole, she liked her life. It was good. Full. And just the way she wanted it. She liked an empty house. The silence. The time to herself.

So why then was she so glad that Rick would be coming over to the house after work?

* * *

The small beach house was just the way he imagined Eileen's place would look. Craftsman style, the front of the house was all wood and aged stone. It had to be at least sixty years old, with charm in the hand-carved porch railings and the stone balustrades.

He parked his luxury sedan at the curb and paused beside his car to take a good look at her place. Just a few blocks inland from the beach, the house was surrounded by greenery and fall flowers. Painted a bright sunshine-yellow with forest-green trim, the cottage looked warm and inviting. White wicker furniture on the porch invited a visit and the porch light gleamed with a soft pink glow. Naturally Eileen wouldn't have just a plain old white bulb in there. She'd go for color.

Reaching into the car, he pulled out the bottle of iced chardonnay he'd brought along, then started up the rosebush-lined walk. He caught himself wondering what colors those now bare roses might be in the summer. But as soon as the thought entered his mind, he dismissed it. He wouldn't be around long enough to find out anyway.

Rick smiled to himself as he climbed the five front steps. The cement had been painted. Somehow, Eileen had laid out a pattern and then painted the porch and steps to look like a faded, flowered Oriental rug. It looked great, but he couldn't help wondering how she'd ever thought of it. Who the hell painted rugs on cement?

The front door opened.

Eileen stood in the open doorway. Her hair was loose, falling around her shoulders in soft red-gold waves. She wore a short white tank top with slender straps and a pair of faded denim shorts. Her feet were bare and her legs looked impossibly long. His mouth watered and he forgot all about the faux rug on the porch. Forgot about the new client he'd picked up over lunch. Forgot about the wine in his hands. All he could focus on was her.

And heaven help him, what she did to him.

"Hi."

She smiled and his breath left him. Her eyes lit up and her features brightened and his blood pumped a little faster. "Hi back," he said.

"That for me?" She indicated the wine.

"Yeah."

"Want some now?" she asked, stepping back to let him in.

"Not thirsty," he said, entering the house, then closing the door behind him.

"Me, neither," she said, taking the wine from him long enough to drop it onto the nearby couch.

"Good," he muttered, and grabbed her, pulling her close, wrapping his arms around her and holding on as if his grip on her meant his life. And maybe, just for the moment, it did.

She went up on her toes and met his kiss coming in. Her lips parted, her breath left her, rushing to him, and his tongue swept into her mouth, instantly demanding, plundering, pushing her back to the brink she now knew so well.

He tore his mouth from hers and laid down a path of hot, damp kisses along the column of her throat. She moaned softly, holding on to his shoulders and arching into him. His hands lifted the hem of her shirt and swept beneath the fabric to cup her breasts, his fingers teasing, tweaking, caressing.

She hissed in a breath through clenched teeth and held it, as if afraid she wouldn't be able to draw another. Rick nibbled at her neck, tasted the frantic pulse beat at the base of her throat, and felt his own heartbeat kick into high gear and match the wild rhythm of hers.

Lifting his head, he continued to palm her breasts, rubbing the tips of her nipples just to watch a glassy sheen dazzle her eyes. ''Bedroom?''

She licked her lips, blinked a couple of times, then tried to focus on his face. Lifting one hand, she pointed. ''Thataway.''

''Let's go,'' he said, and bent low enough to plant one shoulder in her middle. Then he stood up, draping her across one shoulder.

''Hey!'' Both hands on his back, she pushed herself up. ''What's with the caveman routine?''

He gave her behind a friendly swat. ''Quicker this way.''

''Okay then,'' she said, and let herself drop against his back while he crossed the room in a few long strides. ''As long as there's a good reason.''

Rick moved through the living room without even looking at it. Right now, he wasn't interested in the decor. All he was interested in was Eileen. And finding that sweet satisfaction he'd only ever found with her. He needed her, damn it.

He didn't want to.

Hadn't planned to.

But in the space of one long weekend, she'd become... important. His grip on her tightened in response to that thought, but he didn't linger on it. Didn't want to consider what ramifications might be lurking behind that one little word, *important*.

He glanced through one open doorway. Green tiles, parrots in jungle shower curtain. Bathroom.

"Turn left," she said, as he paused in the hallway.

He did.

"No, the other left," she corrected, pushing herself up again. "*My* left. This upside down and backward trying to give directions thing sucks."

"You're a backseat driver, too, aren't you?"

"Only trying to help."

He walked into her bedroom, noted the queen-size bed covered with a pale blue-and-white quilt, and ignored everything else. A small, beside lamp was on, sending a pale yellow light spreading across the blanket. Bending down, he flipped her onto the mattress and she laughed when she landed and bounced a couple of times.

"There's just nothing like a Neanderthal," she said, stretching like a cat on the bed.

"Glad you approve."

"Oh, yeah."

Eileen watched him through eyes already hazy

with a building passion that swamped her with sensation and expectation. He looked...different. He wore a black sweater over dark blue jeans and the casual clothes made him seem more—reachable, somehow. The suits that were such a part of him were almost like a well-cut wall he wore around him, keeping the world at bay. Tonight he'd apparently stopped by his own house to change before coming over. And as much as she appreciated the new him, she wanted him out of those clothes. Now.

As if he heard her thoughts, he tore his sweater off and threw it aside. The glow from the lamp defined his broad chest and Eileen's insides shivered. As he stripped off his jeans, her breath came fast and hard and her body went warm and damp and ready.

He came to her then, kneeling on the bed beside her, lifting her from the mattress slightly to yank her tank top up and over her head. Then he bent to her breasts, taking first one nipple, then the other into his mouth, teasing, tasting, taking them both to the beginning of another wild, fast ride.

Eileen gasped and fought for breath. She ran her fingers through his hair, then skimmed her hands down to stroke his shoulders, his back. He lifted his head, looked into her eyes and admitted, "I missed you, damn it. Even though we worked together all day, I missed you."

"Yeah," she said, and slid one hand around to cup his face in her palm. "I know. I feel the same way."

"Which means…"

"Heck if I know," Eileen said and sucked in a gulp of air when he dropped one hand to the waistband of her shorts. She held that breath while he undid the button, pulled down the zipper, then drew the shorts and her panties down her legs. She kicked free of them, then said, "I just know I want you. Really bad."

His lips curved into a smile that shook her to her toes. "Back atcha, Eyeball."

She laughed as he shifted to cover her body with his. She opened for him, welcoming him as he pushed himself within her. Still smiling, she rocked her hips against his and gave herself up to the wonder he created inside her. She looked up into his eyes and found more than desire written there. She also saw warmth, humor and tenderness.

Sensations spiraled through her and as her peak hovered close, she realized that she and Rick had crossed a border at some point. They'd moved beyond simple passion and hunger to a realm where things could get a lot more complicated.

There was something more here than desire.

How much more, she didn't know.

Then his body pushed her higher, faster and she forgot to think. All she focused on was the moment. This time with him, when it was just the two of them in the soft light, bodies claiming each other, breath mingling in the quiet.

When the first dazzling sparks shot through her bloodstream, she held on to him tightly, digging her short nails into his shoulders. Her voice broke on his name and a moment later, he stiffened against her, finding his own release and following her into the haze of completion. Eileen wrapped her arms around him and held him tightly as together they fell.

Two days later, they were together again in her room, as they had been every moment when they weren't at work. Something was happening between them, but neither of them was willing to admit it, much less talk about it. Instead, they wrapped themselves in the staggering sensations that surrounded them. Losing themselves in the magic. Finding more than they'd bargained for. More than they wanted to claim.

Rick worried that they were getting in too deep, but he couldn't seem to stay away from her. In a rational corner of his mind, a small voice warned him to start distancing himself. To start pulling away, retreating from Eileen and the dangers she represented.

But he couldn't do it.

Not yet.

He would, though. He *had* to. Because no matter what, he wouldn't be drawn into a situation where a woman had the power to crush him again. But there was time. There was still time to enjoy what he'd found before having to give it up.

For now, though, he moved inside her again, rocking his body into hers, driving her and himself to the very edge. Then with one last thrust, Rick felt her body flex around his, watched her eyes widen and heard her whisper his name as the tremors took her—and only then did he allow himself to find the completion he needed so desperately.

Minutes later, he rolled to one side of her, groaned and said, "Damn it."

Eileen gasped, struggling for air as she fought to get her heartbeat back under control. She turned her head to look at him, a satisfied smile on her face. "Rick, what could possibly be wrong?"

His expression tightened as his narrowed gaze locked with hers. "The condom broke."

Her eyes went wide and, even in the dim light, he saw her skin blanch. *"Uh-oh."*

"That about covers it." Dread pooled in the pit of his stomach, but there was still a chance. "Tell me you're on the pill."

"You want me to lie at a time like this?"

"Damn."

"Hey," she said, reaching for the quilt to cover herself, "until you, I hadn't been with anyone in a couple of years." She drew the quilt up over both of them. "I wasn't going to be taking pills when there was no need for them."

"Okay, then." Pushing one hand through his hair, he gritted his teeth and asked, "Let's figure this out. When was your last period?"

Eileen shifted her gaze to the ceiling and tried to focus. Hard to actually think when your body was still churning. But she tried. Thinking back, she counted, mentally tripping over her body's calendar. Then she recounted. And did it one more time. *Oh, God.*

She hesitated, then realized that there was no easy way to say it. "It was, uh, *due* three days ago."

"Uh-oh."

Eight

"How long does it take, anyway?"

Eileen shot Rick a dangerous look. "Three minutes, okay?" She'd already told him that several times, but, apparently, it wasn't getting through. But then, she could sort of understand that. She, too, was feeling a wild mixture of panic and fear and expectation and even, if she was completely honest and why the hell not, since only she would know... *excitement*.

She was about to find out if she was going to be a mother, for Pete's sake. A mother. Her. She'd given up on that particular little dream when she'd found Robert doing the horizontal cha-cha with the bimbo of the week. Eileen loved being an aunt to Bridie's kids, and she'd long told herself that that was enough. That she didn't need to actually give birth to feel complete. But she obviously hadn't believed herself because here she stood, hoping she was pregnant and terrified to admit it.

She pulled in a long, deep breath, let it out slowly, then repeated, "Three minutes."

"Longest three minutes of my life," Rick muttered, and paced the confines of the short hallway outside the bathroom.

"Well, contrary to public opinion," she said as she watched him turn and pace in the other direction, "snapping people's heads off does *not* make time fly."

He stopped and looked at her over his shoulder. "Sorry. It's just…"

"Yeah, I know." Eileen leaned one shoulder against the doorjamb and somehow resisted peeking in the bathroom door at the pregnancy test wand laying on the counter. She'd know soon enough. And when she knew…that would be the time for panic. And decision making. And maybe, for scraping Rick up off the floor.

No, she thought, as she watched him shoving both hands through his hair with enough force to yank every hair out of his head, that wasn't totally fair. He could've split, told her it was her problem to deal with and just disappeared. But he hadn't. Instead, right after discovering the broken condom, he'd gotten dressed, driven to the drugstore and bought a pregnancy test kit. Now he was waiting out the results with her.

Of course, she knew darn well what answer he was hoping for. She could all but see him issuing fervent prayers to the gods of fortune.

"Just because one broke doesn't mean the others were faulty," he said, and she was pretty sure he was talking to himself more than her.

But she answered him anyway. "Condoms aren't a hundred percent effective anyway."

"Thanks for that."

She shrugged and folded her arms across her chest. "I'm just saying—"

"That maybe a stop-and-shop gas station wasn't the *best* place to buy protection?" he finished for her.

Eileen smiled. Her stomach was in knots, her hands were shaking, hence the folded arms thing, after all, why should she advertise her own case of nerves? "The point is, there's no use in rehashing now. Or saying what if. The deed is most definitely done."

"I know," he said, and turning around, leaned back against the wall, his gaze fixed on the bathroom doorway.

When the timer went off, both of them jumped. He took a step, then stopped, letting her go into the room before him. Eileen hit the stop button on the timer first, since the incessant ringing was drilling a hole through her head. She picked up the wand carefully, as if it might explode if handled roughly. Glancing back at him as he came up behind her, she said, "We look together?"

He nodded. "Together."

Staring down at the tiny window where the results were displayed, she saw the tiny pink plus sign. Her stomach fisted. She heard his quick intake of breath. Her fingers tightened on the plastic. "Since it's pink, do you suppose that means it's a girl?"

If he could have figured out how to do it effectively, Rick would've kicked his *own* ass. Stupid, he thought. Stupid and careless and now…caught.

From his chair at the two-person table, he watched Eileen move around the small homey kitchen. She'd already made a pot of coffee and now she busily brought cups and a plateful of homemade chocolate chip cookies to the table. She hadn't said a word in fifteen minutes and the silence was beginning to stretch a little thin. Although, Rick thought, he really couldn't blame her for not speaking. Hell, he couldn't think of anything to say, either. An apology didn't seem right, but congratulations was clearly out of the question, too.

When she finally sat down opposite him, she poured a cup of coffee for each of them, picked up a cookie and proceeded to nervously turn it into crumbs.

Rick reached across the table and covered her hands with his. "We have to talk about this."

Her gaze lifted to his and he tried to read the emotions darting across the meadow-green surface of her eyes. But they shifted and changed so quickly it was impossible to nail one down.

"Look Rick," she said after a long minute, "I know you're trying to help, but honestly, I don't want to talk about it right now."

"But we have some decisions to make." Hell, they had a ton of decisions to make.

She smiled, shook her head and leaned back in the chair. "I'm not deciding anything tonight."

"Eileen, this is serious."

"Really?" She took a bite of her cookie, chewed it and swallowed. "You mean being pregnant isn't a joke? It's not all fun and games? Wow. I'll alert the media."

"Funny."

"Didn't mean to be." She ate the rest of her cookie and reached for another one.

"Is chocolate really the answer?"

"Chocolate can solve just about anything."

"Not this."

"I said, just about. Besides, it's worth a try."

He pushed his chair back and the legs scraped against the worn linoleum with a screech. Standing up, he came around the table, reached down and grabbed her hands, then pulled her to her feet.

Her eyes looked bruised, worried and that ate at him. If she hadn't come to help him out—to do him a favor, they never would have connected again and she wouldn't be standing here pregnant.

With *his* child.

That last sentence bounced around the inside of his heart and cracked the edges of it just a little. A child. He'd never expected to be a father. Well, certainly not after his wife had left him. When he first got married, he'd convinced himself that he was in love. That he and Allison would build a family together. But then in a few short months, he'd discovered that Allison had had her eye on his bank account, not their future.

When she left, his dreams had died. And out of the ashes, he'd built a new company and a new life for himself. If that life was a little lonelier than he'd once imagined he would be, at least it was a fair trade-off. He'd never have to watch another woman walk out of his life.

Now, suddenly, the rules had changed on him again. Now there was a tiny life inside Eileen that existed because of *him*. Whether or not they'd wanted this to happen, it *had*. And he wouldn't brush it aside. Wouldn't walk away. He'd be damned if he'd abandon his own child as his parents had done to him.

And since walking away wasn't an option, there was only one thing left.

"Eileen," he said, staring down into the eyes that had haunted him since first seeing her walk into his office more than a week ago, "marry me."

She blinked, shook her head and blinked again. *"What?"*

"You heard me."

"I know what I think I heard, but pregnancy must affect your hearing." She tried to pull away from him, but he held her tight. "You're just reacting— you're not thinking rationally."

He laughed shortly and let her go. "You? Teaching me about rational?"

"Somebody has to." Eileen reached up and scooped her hair back from her face. She felt trapped. Standing with her back to the wall, the fridge on one side of her, the table on the other and Rick blocking the way out, she suddenly couldn't catch her breath. Pent-up emotions charged through her body, closing her throat and sheening her eyes with tears she didn't want to cry.

She needed time to herself to figure this out. To deal with everything that was crowding her mind and her heart. She was pregnant. She had a baby inside her. Living. Growing. Oh, my.

"Marry you?" she repeated, and pushed him out of her way so she could walk past him, "God, Rick. I'm about ten minutes pregnant and you want to plan a wedding?"

"It's the right thing to do."

"Sure," she said over her shoulder as she stalked into the living room, "if you're living in a movie from the fifties."

He was right behind her. And suddenly, her living room seemed a lot smaller than usual.

Grabbing her forearm, he turned her around to face him. "Eileen, that's *my* baby you're carrying."

"Rick, it's too soon to talk about this." She needed quiet. She needed to think. To feel. To plan. Good God. She, Eileen Ryan, needed a plan? The woman who hadn't planned anything in years? If she wasn't so scared, she might have laughed at the idea.

"Fine," he said, and let her go, taking a step backward as if to keep himself from reaching for her again. "It's too soon. But—" he waited for her to meet his gaze before continuing "—I have to know you'll talk to me before you decide anything."

His features were taut, strained, and Eileen knew he was feeling the same turmoil racing through her, so she smiled as she reached up to cup his face in her palm. "I promise. Just…give me a little time, okay?"

A few hours later, Eileen let herself into Larkspur, shutting the front door quietly behind her. Instantly she was enveloped in the commingled perfume of flowers. The scents of chrysanthemums, roses, sweet peas and dozens of others filled the small shop.

Strings of tiny white lights outlined the two large windows that fronted Pacific Coast Highway and threw shadows around the small showroom. Galvanized buckets of water crouched in the center of the room, holding the flowers that didn't need refrigeration to retain their freshness. Across the room were the glass refrigerator cases, where the roses, orchids and other more fragile flowers stood waiting their chance to be admired.

She hit the overhead light switch and a bank of fluorescent lights flickered to life, dropping shadows around the room. Eileen walked into the back room where the florist supplies were kept. Glass vases in varied shapes and sizes and colors were stacked on a series of shelves. Nearby, there was florists tape and shears and green foam and everything else required to build the fantasy flower arrangements Larkspur was known for.

Everything was neat as a pin. The floor was freshly swept and the cuttings from the day had been carried out to the trash can behind the shop.

Flipping on the radio, Eileen listened to a slow, sad song about love and loss. Then she shrugged out of her sweatshirt and reached for one of the vases. Working with the flowers always relaxed her, gave her a chance to think. To let her mind wander while her hands were busy.

And boy, did she need to think.

Rick's apartment was dark. Empty. He stood with his back to the room, staring out a bank of windows at the ocean below. Off shore, oil derrick islands were lit up like a tropical paradise and a few boats bobbed in the harbor, their running lights twinkling on the dark surface of the water.

The quiet was starting to get to him. But he was used to being alone and he couldn't remember it bothering him much before this past week and a half.

Now, whenever he was in this place, all he could think about was leaving it. Going to work, where he'd see Eileen—or better yet, going to her house, where he could be with her. Being there, in her house, he felt…alive. There was warmth there. And laughter. There were long hours cuddled together on her couch watching old movies. There was music, drifting from her neighbor's backyard and the sound of kids playing hoops down the street.

Here…he turned from the windows and raked his gaze across the narrow, sparsely furnished room. After his divorce, he'd moved into this apartment, thinking it was a temporary thing. Then the days and weeks and months had slipped past and he'd stopped thinking about moving. Stopped living—beyond his work. Until Eileen.

Fear chewed at his insides, though he didn't want to admit it even to himself. When she left, as he knew she would, she'd not only be taking the warmth he'd only just discovered—she'd be taking his child.

He couldn't allow that.

Taking a sip of his twelve-year-old Scotch, he felt the fiery liquid spill heat throughout his body and knew it wouldn't last. The chill gripping him since leaving Eileen was bone deep.

And it was only going to get worse.

The ball whizzed past his opponent's ear and Rick winced as the man ducked. "Sorry."

"Man, who're you trying to kill?" Mike Taylor asked. "Me? Or just a poor innocent ball?"

"Neither," Rick said, and stalked to the sidelines where he'd dropped his towel and a quart-sized bottle of water.

The early morning game of racquetball wasn't going so well. He'd thought that a quick game would clear his head. That working up a sweat would somehow help him clear things in his mind. But it wasn't working. Hell, he wasn't even winning. Usually he was way ahead of Mike by now. Instead, he was six points behind and fading fast.

Wiping his face with the towel, he slung it over his left shoulder and watched his friend approach. He and Mike had been college roommates. And that was the only thing they had in common. Rick studied the market and Mike built custom motorcycles for the idle rich. He was so damn good at it, he'd become rich himself—though far from idle. He still built the bikes himself, preferring to stay in the "pit" as he called it.

"So what's goin' on?" Mike reached out for his bottle of water and unscrewed the cap.

"Nothing."

"Sure." Mike took a long drink, then capped the bottle again. "You never play this bad, man. Something's on your mind."

Rick looked at his old friend for a long minute. "I asked Eileen Ryan to marry me."

Mike was so damn impassive, Rick wasn't really sure his friend had heard him. Until he said, "Are you nuts?"

"Entirely possible," Rick muttered.

"Thought you swore off marriage after Allison left you bloody and broke."

"I did."

Mike snorted a laugh and slung his towel around

his neck. "Proposing's a weird way to avoid marriage, man."

"She's pregnant."

Mike's blue eyes went wide as he scraped one hand across his jaw. "You sure it's yours?"

That was the one worry that had never crossed his mind. Eileen was too honest and outspoken to lie about something like this.

"Yeah, I'm sure."

Mike nodded. "Is she keeping the baby?"

"Don't know." Rick shifted his gaze toward the plate-glass wall that divided this racquetball court from the one beside it. The gym was crowded, with everyone trying to get in a workout before heading off to their jobs. But he wasn't paying attention to the people surrounding him. Instead, his mind was focused, as it had been all during the sleepless night, on Eileen. And his child.

He'd never wanted to be a father, but now that the baby existed, he couldn't stand the idea of losing it. And if she decided to end this pregnancy, there wasn't a damn thing he could do about it. His hands fisted helplessly at his sides.

He didn't want a wife.

But he damn sure wanted his child.

By the end of the week, Rick was holding on to his unraveling temper with a tight fist. Somehow or other, Eileen had managed to avoid him for the last few days. Oh, she showed up for work every morning, right on time. She was polite, efficient, and completely shut him out anytime he tried to talk to her about what was happening. About the baby. About them. Hell. About anything other than work.

Rick had tried to give her space. He'd swallowed his impatience and buried his concerns. He looked into her soft green eyes and read no welcome there, so he didn't force the issue. He hadn't stopped by her place after work, even though it was killing him to stay away. He missed her, damn it. He'd driven down her street and paused long enough to look at her lamp-lit windows, but he hadn't stopped, not sure if he'd be welcome or not. And to be honest, he didn't think he'd be able to stand it if she opened the door and told him to leave.

But he'd waited as long as he could. Today was the last day she'd be working for him. By Monday, he'd have some anonymous temp in the outer office and Eileen would be back in her flower shop—as far away from his world as if she were on Saturn.

So it was now or never. Standing up from behind his desk, he crossed the room and stood in the open doorway leading to the outer office. Eileen had been here only two short weeks, but her presence had been made known. There were sweet-smelling flowers in a glass bowl on her desk, colorful throw pillows on the plain, dark blue couch and a small watercolor in a pale yellow frame hung near the file cabinets. With just a few minor changes, she'd lightened up his reception room—made it more welcoming for clients.

Just as, simply by being *her,* she'd made changes in his life.

He used to be content to spend his evenings alone, mapping out the next day's work. He'd focused all of his energies on the business that had been his whole life. Now, when he wasn't with Eileen, he was thinking about her. He couldn't sleep at night because her image kept him awake. His bed felt empty and the quiet was deafening. He'd never considered having a family—now he was worried about a baby that wasn't even the size of a pencil eraser.

His gaze locked on Eileen as she sat with her back to him, the phone held to her left ear. Morning sunlight drifted through the tinted windows and lay over her like a gentle haze. She almost seemed dreamlike. But Rick knew, only too well, just how real she was.

"Okay, Paula," she was saying. "I'll be back at the shop on Monday."

Monday, he thought, realizing that was just a few days away. When she wasn't here, in the office every day, how would he get her to talk to him? How would he prevent her from slipping out of his life and taking his child with her?

"That's great!" Eileen's voice hit a high note. "The Baker wedding? That's terrific."

Joy filled her voice, and when she laughed it was like music. Rick leaned against the doorjamb and folded his arms over his chest, just enjoying the sound of it. When she was gone, the emptiness she'd leave behind would be impossible to fill. Damn it, she hadn't even left him yet and he already missed her.

Eileen half turned in her chair to reach for a pad and a pen. That's when she spotted him. "Um, Paula? I'll call you back later, okay?" She smiled into the phone, shifting her gaze from his. "Yeah, I'll do that. Okay. Bye."

He waited until she hung up. "Paula?"

"She's the manager of my flower shop."

Rick didn't give a good damn who Paula was, but at least Eileen was talking to him. "Problem?"

"No," she said, and turned away, rummaging through her desk aimlessly. Finally she grabbed another of the chocolates Margo had left behind and quickly unwrapped it. Popping it into her mouth, she bit down hard and said, "Actually, it's good news. We landed a big wedding."

"Congratulations."

"Thanks." Her fingers twisted the scrap of silver foil candy wrapper.

She wouldn't even look at him and the tether on Rick's temper strained to the breaking point. "I'm the boss here," he said. "You can't ignore me."

She glanced at him, then away again. "I'm not ignoring you, I'm *overlooking* you. There's a difference."

"Funny, feels the same."

"Yeah, I guess it would."

He came away from the doorway, walked up behind her and gave her chair a spin hard enough to turn her around.

"Talk to me," he said.

She nodded and stood up to face him. She was close, really close. Trapped between the chair and his body. Typical Eileen, she didn't try to run, just stood her ground. She reached up, and for a split second he thought she was going to touch his face and his heart stopped. But all she did was tuck her hair behind her ears, displaying her simple silver hoop earrings. They winked at him in the sunlight. "You're crowding me," she said, then reached out and casually pushed against his chest until he stepped back out of her way. "I appreciate you not pushing me this week, Rick."

"It wasn't easy."

"I can see that," she said, and lifted one hand to briefly touch his cheek. "You look like you're ready to implode."

He blew out a breath, pushed his suit jacket back and shoved his hands into his pants pockets. "Close."

"Well, don't. Everything's fine. Or—" she thought about it for a moment "—*will* be fine. I'm keeping the baby."

Rick's heart started beating again. Now that he knew that, the rest would fall into place. It would be all right. "So you'll marry me."

Nine

Eileen blinked at him. In the past few days, she'd thought about little else but the baby inside her and the panicked proposal he'd made. She was positive it had been nothing more than a knee-jerk reaction to a situation neither of them had been prepared for. In those first few hours, she'd actually considered what it might have been like if he'd *meant* that proposal. If he'd really loved her. If they'd met, and fallen in love and *then* slept together and *then* got married and *then* got pregnant.

Briefly she'd entertained the image of she and Rick and baby made three, all living happily ever after in her tiny cottage in Laguna. But reality had reared its ugly head in time to splinter that vision and remind her that a temporary affair wasn't exactly the best basis for a marriage even if Rick *had* meant the proposal.

And of course he hadn't. It was a knee-jerk reaction. Which said a lot, she guessed, about his character. But she didn't want to be the good deed he was forcing himself to do.

"You have to stop saying that," she said.

"I want to help."

"Helping is doing the dishes, not proposing."

"I don't do dishes."

Eileen smiled. "Cute, but I'm still not marrying you."

Frustration rippled across his features and was gone again in the next instant as he tried a different approach. "What about the baby? Are you…"

She dropped one hand to her flat belly in a protective gesture that he noted with one raised eyebrow. "I'm going to raise it myself."

"I'm glad." Then his features tightened and his eyes narrowed. "But it's my child, too."

"Yes, but right now, it's more mine than yours."

"And I have no say in anything."

"I didn't say that, exactly."

"I won't be shut out, Eileen."

Eileen bent down to open the bottom desk drawer and pull her purse from its depths. Flipping back the leather flap, she dug into the big, dark brown bag and rummaged around for her keys. While she searched, she talked. "We both went into this saying no strings. Remember? And either one of us could end it whenever we were ready?"

"That was then," Rick said tightly. "This is now. It's not just us anymore. There's a baby involved. And strings don't come any bigger than that."

Her fingers curled around her car keys as she pulled them slowly from her bag. Lifting her gaze to his, she fought down a pang of something she really didn't want to look at too closely. But how could she not? Once again, she wasn't wanted for *herself*. Rick didn't want to marry her because he was crazy in love. Not even because he couldn't live without her in his bed. Nope. He only wanted her because she was carrying his child. Admitting that to herself stung, but better that she face the truth, which was that *nobody* needed that kind of marriage.

"True. But a baby isn't enough of a reason to get married."

A harsh laugh shot from his throat, but no humor shone in his eyes as he scraped one hand through his hair. As if he couldn't stand still, he stalked off a pace or two, then spun around and came right back. "Funny. That's what my parents thought, too."

Eileen winced at the echo of old pain coloring his voice. His eyes were filled with shadows that tore at her even as she sensed the emotional distance he was keeping between them. He didn't want her pity, but she couldn't help the tide of sympathy that rose up inside her. "Rick…"

"They didn't bother to get married. They didn't bother to raise me, either." His jaw tightened and as he continued speaking, Eileen could almost *feel* him pulling away from her. "They handed me off to my grandmother and went their separate ways."

"Rick, I'm sorry."

His gaze snapped to meet hers. "I don't need your pity, thanks. What I want is to be my child's father."

Eileen reached out and laid one hand on his forearm, somehow wanting to reassure the boy he'd once been—along with the man standing in front of her. "You will be. You just won't be married to its mother."

A few hours later, curled up on her couch, Eileen tried again, as she had for the past few days, to come to grips with what had happened. In the course of a couple of short weeks, she'd reconnected with Rick, found the lover of her dreams and wound up pregnant. That had to be some sort of record.

Dipping her spoon into the monster-sized chocolate sundae she'd made for herself, she scooped up the whipped cream and chocolate sprinkles and savored the rich, smooth taste. Wouldn't you know, she thought, that she'd set *this* kind of record? "You couldn't just jump rope for a hundred and eighty-seven days straight?" she muttered.

She stabbed her spoon into the ice cream and remembered the look on Rick's face when she'd walked out of the office, leaving him alone. She'd chanced one last look at his face—saw the loneliness and resignation in his eyes, and had almost gone rushing back to him. Almost.

But she'd remembered the one important point.

He didn't want her for her.

He wanted her for the baby within her.

Disappointment welled up like a wave surging toward shore. Maybe if he'd proposed differently. Maybe if he'd told her that what they had was more than physical. Maybe if he'd—

A knock on the door had her jumping and twisting in her seat to stare at it. *Rick?* Her stomach skittered nervously and she was torn between pleasure and impatience that he'd show up at the house to plead his case again. She didn't want to keep saying no, but she couldn't very well say yes to a man who didn't actually *want* her, could she? More brisk knocking sounded out and Eileen told herself she'd just ignore it. After all, just because someone dropped by didn't mean she had to pay attention.

"Eileen Honora Ryan!" Her grandmother's voice rang out loud and clear. "You open this door right this minute."

Scrambling, Eileen set the sundae on the coffee table and raced around the edge of the couch. Grabbing the doorknob, she turned it and yanked the door open, narrowly missing being rapped on the nose by Maggie Ryan's knuckles. "Gran? What's wrong?"

The older woman's face was flushed, cheeks pink, eyes flashing. She pushed into the house, shooting Eileen a look that she hadn't seen since junior high when she'd toilet-papered her history teacher's house. "Gran?" Her gaze followed the older woman as she stomped into the living room, turned around and glared.

"What do you mean you won't marry Rick Hawkins?"

Eileen closed the door, barely managing to keep from slamming it. *Big mouth.* And a dirty fighter. Going behind her back to her grandmother was cheating and he knew it.

"He told you."

Her grandmother sniffed, put both hands on her hips and tapped the toe of one shoe against the braided rug. "He did the honorable thing. He came to your family, explained the situation and told me he wants to marry you."

"Because of the baby."

"Precisely."

"No way." Eileen swallowed hard, but she wouldn't give in on this. "I'm not going to marry a man who doesn't want me. All he's concerned about is the baby. This isn't about *me* at all." She reached up and tightened the rubber band around her ponytail. Then she shifted a quick look at her grandmother before looking away. "It's Robert all over again, Gran. Robert wanted me so I could support him and Rick wants the baby."

Gran's eyes softened. "Ah…I think I understand."

"What?" Eileen kept a wary eye on her grandmother. An abrupt change of heart like that could only mean she'd thought of a better plan of attack. It paid to keep on your toes around Maggie Ryan.

"Well, if you didn't love him, you'd marry him."
Her grandmother shrugged slightly. "He's a rich,
handsome, kind man, with whom you *obviously*
share an…affection. So, if your heart weren't involved, you'd accept his proposal, because you'd
risk nothing." She smiled and folded her hands at
her waist. "But caring for him, you risk pain. So
you must actually love Rick—or at least be *falling*
in love with him."

She swayed a little, as if she'd taken a direct hit.
Love? No one had said anything about *love.*

"That's ridiculous." Eileen walked around the
couch, plopped down and reached for her sundae
again. Love? She liked him. A lot, actually. He
made her laugh. He was fun to talk to. He was smart.
And kind. And—enough, she ordered herself. She
wasn't in love with a man who didn't love her back.
She wouldn't do that. Not again. Taking a huge bite
of her sundae, she winced as an ice cream headache
instantly throbbed between her eyes. Great. Now
even her snack was ruined. She set the ice cream
back on the table and squinted at her grandmother
as she rubbed her forehead.

"I'm not in love with him and I'm not going to
marry him just because you and he think it's a swell
idea."

"I raised you better than this, Eileen." Simple
words, spoken in a soft, disappointed voice. "Your
baby deserves better."

"My baby will have me, and you, and Bridie."

Her sister Bridget would be delighted to be able to love a baby she didn't have to deliver herself.

"And a father? What about the baby's father?"

The father? When Eileen caught up to him, the baby's father was going to pay for spilling his guts to Gran.

Rick knew before he even answered the door that it would be Eileen. When he'd gone to see Maggie after work, he'd realized that he was setting himself up for a hell of a fight with Eileen. But even being prepared, he was taken aback by the dangerous glint in her eyes as she glared at him before stomping past him into the living room. She stood in the middle of the lamplit room, the night beyond the windows black and empty.

As empty as he'd felt since the moment she'd walked out of the office. Out of his world.

"That was low, Hawkins," Eileen said as she whirled around, strawberry ponytail flying to smack her across the eyes. "Going to Gran was really low."

"Yeah, I know." He closed the door and walked into the room, hands stuffed into his pants pockets so he wouldn't be tempted to reach out and grab her. "Desperate times…"

"You fight dirty," she snapped, interrupting him. "I'll have to remember that."

"You left me no choice." He'd have used whatever weapons he had at his disposal to convince her.

He couldn't let this go. Couldn't walk away and pretend everything was fine.

"But going to Gran? I wouldn't have thought you'd—" she said, letting her gaze sweep the sterile room. He looked at it through her eyes and watched her note the plain, unadorned furniture. The barren walls, lack of anything even remotely homey. "This place is awful."

"Yes, I went to your grandmother—and the place isn't that bad."

"The decorator ought to be shot."

"There was no decorator."

"*You* did this?" She turned in a half circle, and he watched her, as she shook her head in disbelief. "It's like a hotel room—no wait. Hotel rooms have color." She looked at him again. "You're taking this little gray world of yours *way* too far."

"I'm not here a lot."

"Good thing. You'd stick your head in the oven."

"It's electric."

"Probably safer that way." She shook her head again and then got back on track. "Anyway, the point is, I'm not going to marry you just because you sicced Gran on me."

"Damn it, Eileen," he said, stalking closer, unable to keep his distance, or his temper. "I don't want my child born a bastard."

She flinched and pulled her head back to stare at him openmouthed. "That's an ugly word. And an outdated one."

He barked a laugh that scraped his throat and tore at his heart. "It's so easy for someone like you."

"What?"

"Your grandmother raised you and Bridget. But your parents were married. They loved you guys. The only reason you didn't grow up with them is because they died."

Eileen blanched a little at the old yet still painful memory.

"Your parents loved you two. They were *married.* Committed to each other and their children." Rick, on the other hand, knew just how cruel other children could be. "You don't know. That word's not so outdated," he muttered, his hands fisting in his pockets.

Her voice dropped too, as she said, "Our child will be fine. Loved. It won't matter—"

His gaze snapped to hers. "It'll matter to *me,*" he ground out. "And trust me, it'll matter to him, when kids start calling him names."

"They won't."

"They will." Staring into her eyes, he swallowed a hard knot of bitterness choking his throat. "You don't know what that's like, Eileen. But I do. I remember. And I won't let a child of mine experience the same damn thing."

"Rick—"

"Being married to me wouldn't be so bad," he said, rushing to convince her. Hell, he was a rich man. He could give her whatever she wanted. "I could help you expand your flower shop..."

"I don't need—"

"You were talking about that wedding job you got earlier—" he said, warming to his theme now. If he couldn't get her to marry him for the child's sake, maybe she'd marry him if he could show her what he could do for her. Hell, Allison had married him for his money. Why not Eileen?

But no. Eileen was nothing like Allison. She wouldn't care if he was broke or a gazillionaire. She was smart and funny and so damn independent she didn't *need* him at all. Money wouldn't convince her. But maybe he could talk her into marrying him just for the sake of their child. Of course, he knew she wouldn't stay with him. She'd never stay. Not forever. But before she left, they could be married and give their child a name. Protect it from the hurts other kids could, and would, deliver. "I could help there, too. Finance you and you could go into the wedding planner business. You'd be good at it."

"Rick," she said on a sigh, "I like my business just the way it is."

He kept talking though, pointing out all the ways that being married would be a good thing. Which wasn't easy, since he'd hardly had a stellar experience with it himself.

Eileen listened, but more importantly, she *heard* him. He was talking so fast, she was pretty sure even *he* wasn't sure of everything he was saying. But she understood. It wasn't *just* the baby motivating him. It was more. She knew why he was so determined to marry her. Whether he knew it or not, he did care for her. Oh, he'd never admit it, but he did. It was there in his eyes. Along with the fear that she was slipping away from him.

As had everyone else in his life.

Except for the grandmother who'd raised him, no one he'd cared about had ever stayed.

His parents.

His ex-wife.

Now he was sure *she* was leaving, too.

So he was protecting himself and his child the only way he knew how. Her heart ached for him as understanding dawned and a million thoughts careened through her mind at once. Maybe Gran was right, she thought. Maybe she *did* love him. If she didn't, she could marry him with a clear conscience—make it a sort of business deal.

But since she *did* care, she *couldn't* marry him? Okay, next stop…therapy. She was getting too confused. He wasn't offering her love, because he didn't believe in it. He wasn't offering to be with her always because he believed she wouldn't stay.

So all she could do now, she told herself, was say yes. Because the only way she could convince him that she would stay was by marrying him and proving it to him. The only way he would allow himself to love her was if she could show him that it was safe.

One of them had to take a chance.

And it looked as if it was going to be her.

"Okay," she said, cutting into his speech.

"Okay?" He looked at her, suspicion in his eyes.

Clearly this wasn't going to be easy. But with the decision made, Eileen suddenly knew it was exactly the right thing to do.

"I'll marry you," she said. "On one condition."

Wary, he asked, "What?"

"That it's a *real* marriage. In every way."

He pulled his hands from his pockets and reached for her. Dropping both hands onto her shoulders, he looked down into her eyes and nodded. "A real marriage. For as long as it lasts."

"Well, there's that optimistic outlook again," she said as his arms came around her. Eileen laid her head on his chest, closed her eyes and hoped to hell she was doing the right thing.

The wedding itself was short and sweet. What it lacked in magic, it more than made up for in kitsch.

Plastic ribbons dotted the "pews" and elevator music streamed from the overhead speakers. Happy couples were lined up in the lobby, waiting their turn at the "altar"—a silk-flower-bedecked wicker arch at the end of a narrow red-carpeted aisle. The minister was short and round, with wire-rimmed glasses and a long white beard. Actually, he could have passed for Santa, except for his Hawaiian shirt, faded jeans and sandals.

Both grandmothers were there along with Bridie and her husband. They'd left all three kids with his mother so they could enjoy a long weekend alone in Las Vegas.

Everything was as it should be. Until "Santa"

asked, "Do you take this man to be your lawfully wedded husband?"

Eileen experienced a moment of sheer, undiluted panic. Everything inside her was screaming for her to rethink this situation. It was only two weeks since Rick's hasty proposal and she was sure they were rushing blindly into something that had every possibility of ripping their bleeding hearts from their chests and stomping them into the ground.

She swallowed hard and glanced over her shoulder at her family. Gran, calm and regal as always, looking confused in her dark blue suit with a flashing silver pin on the lapel. Bridie, her red hair shining in the overhead lights, clung to her husband's arm and made wild gestures with her eyes, as if telling Eileen to say *something*. Rick's grandmother, one long, silver braid laying across her right shoulder, chanted quietly.

"Eileen…" Gran whispered the word loudly, as if trying to snap Eileen out of a trance.

"Is everything all right?" Rick's grandmother's hushed stage whisper carried over the numbingly generic music.

All right? Eileen thought. Probably not. She had the distinct feeling that this wedding was going to create more problems than it solved. So what was she doing here?

Eileen looked at the minister, then shifted her gaze to Rick. Her stomach did a slow roller-coaster ride. One look from him turned her insides to jelly and stole her breath. His dark brown eyes met hers, and she saw a mixture of sorrow and acceptance glimmering in their depths. He *expected* her to back out. He was already prepared for her to change her mind and walk away. Heck, a part of him was *waiting* for her to leave him standing alone at the altar.

And that, more than anything, convinced her that she was doing the right thing. "I do," she said.

A flicker of surprise lit his eyes as he slipped a four-karat stone, deep set into a platinum band, onto her finger. Eileen blew out a long breath as she experienced the weight of that ring on her hand. Promises she'd never thought she'd make echoed over and over in her mind. She tried to figure out how a temporary job had slowly worked into a lifetime commitment—and she wondered if it had been *meant* to work out this way. Was she, all those years ago, when Rick Hawkins had been teasing her and cutting off Barbie's head, already destined to reach this day? Had she always been meant to find a future with Rick? Or was it all just a quirk of fate?

She watched the play of light across the surface of the diamond while the minister droned on. And silently she promised the child within her to make this marriage work. To find a way to convince Rick Hawkins that she loved him.

The world went suddenly still.

It was as if time stopped.

She *did* love him.

It wasn't affection. It wasn't just caring.

She was in love. For the first time in her life. With a man who was convinced she already had one foot out the door.

Ten

Time started up again when the minister said, "You can kiss her now, son."

Rick turned her face up to his and lowered his head until they were nose to nose. She held her breath and felt the soft brush of his on her cheeks. Unexpectedly, tears rose up behind her eyes and she blinked frantically to keep them at bay.

While the music played and their families applauded, he whispered, in a voice low enough that only she could hear, "Thanks for this, Eyeball," just before he kissed her.

The moment his lips touched hers, Eileen's heart quickened. Here was magic. Here was thunder and lightning and a rush of blood that made her head swim. Love swelled inside her and she reached up, wrapping her arms around his neck. The warm, solid strength of him pressed against her, felt good... right. She gave herself up to the kiss that seared her soul and stirred up longings for more. Eileen wanted his love. Not just his name. Not just his child.

She wanted him to love her.

To believe in the life they could build together.

And she knew she was in for the fight of her life.

Ignoring their audience and the cluster of couples waiting to be married, Rick took his time about kissing her. He parted her lips with his tongue and she melted into him, savoring the flash of fireworks in her bloodstream and the thundering pound of her heartbeat. Clinging to him, she gave him all that she had, pouring her heart and soul into the kiss—hoping he would feel it, sense it, and know that she wouldn't leave him. Ever.

"Okay folks," the minister said gruffly. "I've got five more couples to marry before dinner, so let's move it along, huh?"

Rick broke the kiss, lifting his head to stare down at her. And just for a minute, Eileen saw something in his eyes that made her feel better about this wedding.

While she accepted congratulations and hugs from her grandmother and sister, she clung to the *hope* she'd read in his eyes and told herself that it was, at least, a start.

At night, Las Vegas sparkled like a black bowl full of precious gems. Ruby, emerald, sapphire and diamond lights lit the darkness until it was as bright as day, yet still disguised the city in a cloak of beauty.

Tourists streamed up and down the sidewalks as traffic stalled on the strip. On one street, you could find the Eiffel Tower, downtown New York and a slice of Italy. You could visit the pyramids, Medieval Europe and the Caesars of Rome. All along the street, crowds of people moved in a hurry, clutching plastic buckets filled with quarters and nickels and what was left of their dreams. Would-be millionaires stepped off curbs into traffic, following the lure of the next casino.

But the view from a penthouse suite was all lights and glory.

Eileen turned away from the window and faced Rick as he closed the door behind the room service waiter. Now that they were alone, their families off and playing somewhere in Sin City, the silence was nearly deafening.

"Hungry?" he asked, lifting the silver dome off one of the plates on the rolling tray.

She hugged herself, rubbing her hands up and down her upper arms. "Not really."

He set the dome back. "Me, neither." Instead, he grabbed a bottle from its silver ice-filled bucket and twisted the wires around its neck. "We'll have some of this instead."

"I probably shouldn't have any." Too bad, she thought, because if there was ever a time when she really wanted a drink, it was now.

"No problem," he said, tearing the wire cage off and tossing it onto the cart. "It's sparkling cider."

Eileen laughed shortly. She shouldn't have been surprised. Of course Rick would remember that she shouldn't have wine—and being him, Mr. Organization, naturally he'd arrange for something appropriate. Warmth trickled through her. "Cider?"

He shrugged. "How bad can it be?"

"Guess we'll find out." While he took care of the bottle, she shifted her gaze to the room. It was huge. A one-bedroom suite with a gigantic living room, it perched on the thirtieth floor of the Sandalwood hotel. Twin sofas sat facing each other, with a wide, low table boasting an arrangement of fresh, fragrant roses in between. A gas fireplace, flames dancing on the faux hearth, was on one wall and a wide entertainment system on the other. A bank of floor-to-ceiling windows opened onto the night and even this high up, the lights from the city below stained the room with a soft glow, making lamplight unnecessary.

Eileen shifted her gaze to the door on the far wall, through which lay the bedroom, where the king-size bed had already been turned down for them by the maid. Her stomach skittered as the image of Rick and her rolling across that wide mattress rose up in her mind. Silly really, but she was nervous. Rick had seen and explored every inch of her body already, so there was no reason for her to be a shy bride, but apparently logic had little to do with how she was feeling.

The cork popped, bounced off the ceiling and landed on one of the couches and Eileen jumped, startled. Slapping one hand to her chest, she blew out a breath and told herself to get a grip. But in another minute or two, Rick was walking toward her, carrying two crystal flutes, filled with the sparkling cider. And just like that, her heart jumped again.

Handing her one of the glasses, he touched his to hers with a quiet *clink* and said, "Here's to us."

She stared up into his eyes and wished he'd meant that. Wished he'd believed that this was the beginning for them instead of the beginning of the end. She wished he could believe that they could build a family. That with love, anything was possible. But all she could hope for was that he'd learn. That she'd be able to convince him that a future was possible. That it was safe to love her.

But Rome hadn't been built in a day, so she would take it slow and try not to lose patience. Though she had the distinct impression that Rick was going to be a lot tougher work than any old Romans had ever had to deal with.

"Right. To us." She nodded and took a long drink, letting the fizzy cider slide down her throat. Her gaze locked on the simple gold band she'd placed on his finger and in the pit of her stomach, worry fizzed along with the cider.

Rick watched the flashing change of emotions charging across the surface of her eyes. And not for the first time since she'd walked back into his life, he wondered what the hell she was thinking. Was she already regretting agreeing to this? Was she already mentally packing her bags?

And why did it matter?

They were married now. His child was protected. No one could ever call him a bastard. Even if Eileen walked out on him tonight, the marriage certificate would be a shield for his child.

But damn it, he didn't want her to leave.

Just the thought of Eileen walking out of his life was enough to open up a black hole of emptiness inside him. When Allison had left him, Rick had survived. She'd hurt him. Disappointed him. But she'd left his heart intact.

When Eileen left, she would take his heart with her.

But for now, she was here and she was his wife. And tonight, was their wedding night.

Taking her glass from her, he set them both aside on a nearby table. Then turning back to her, he cupped her cheek in his palm and asked, "Did I tell you how beautiful you looked today?"

One corner of her mouth lifted. "I don't think so."

"You do," he said, and let his gaze slide down and back up her body, appreciating her beauty now as much as he had when she'd first entered the chapel. The lemon-yellow dress she wore looked like sunshine. Bright and warm, the fabric fell into a full skirt that stopped just above her knees and swirled around her with every step. The neckline was wide, displaying her collarbones and the fine column of her throat to perfection. He'd taken one look at her and felt a flash of something red-hot surge through him. She tossed her head, sending that gorgeous hair of hers into a rippling arc around her head and he'd wanted to go out and find a dragon to slay for her.

As she walked up that short aisle toward him, Rick had told himself to enjoy the sight of her, the picture she made. The anticipation and joy in her face, despite her obvious reservations. He told himself to carve this memory and any others they might make, deeply into his brain, so that they'd always be there, just a dream away.

She smiled at their families as she moved to join him and, when she took her place beside him, an unexpectedly sharp, sweet sting of regret shot through him. Regret that this moment couldn't last.

Already Rick knew that this marriage would end, so it was hard to hold on to any rays of hope, no matter how tempting. Hadn't he been crushed by misplaced hopes before? Hadn't he decided long ago to not be led down the path of impossible dreams?

And yet, when he slipped his ring onto her finger, he realized sadly that he was closer than he'd ever been to *real* love.

But it was too tenuous to hold on to and he could already feel it slipping through his fingers.

She was going to leave.

If not today, then soon. So he couldn't allow himself the luxury of loving her.

But he could give in to the desire raging through him. The need to touch, to caress, to claim.

His thumb moved over her mouth, and his body tightened. Mind racing, pulse pounding, breath staggering from his lungs, Rick watched as her eyes closed and she turned her head into his caress. His fingers touched her smooth, soft skin. In the reflected light of the neon world thirty stories below them, her flesh looked like golden honey and he hungered for her as if it had been years rather than weeks since he'd last touched her.

"I need you," he said softly, not really sure if he'd spoken the words aloud—because they were repeating over and over inside his mind, like a tape stuck in permanent rewind.

"I need you, too," she said, and moved into him, pressing her body along his, inflaming them both.

"Now." Rick took her face between his palms, letting his fingers spear through her long, loose hair at her temples, and the red-gold strands lay across his skin like cool silk.

He kissed her, taking her mouth, plundering her warmth and drawing it deep inside him, where the cold still lurked in the dark corners of his heart. He held her, pressing her tightly to him, as if he could pull her into his body, making her a part of him.

She moved in even closer, as if sensing his need and sharing it. She cupped the back of his head in her palm and kissed him back, showing him her hunger, her need, and Rick reveled in it. Her hands slid across his back, stroking, caressing and all he could think was that there were too many clothes in the way of claiming her.

Reaching behind her, he undid the zipper of her dress and as the fabric spilled away, his fingertips wandered down her spine. She wore no bra and her panties were nothing more than a tiny piece of elastic with a scrap of lace attached. In seconds, they were gone, the elastic snapped in his eagerness to touch her. To hold her. To claim her one more time. To feel all of the things he'd only discovered in her arms.

"Rick—" She broke the kiss with a gasp and breathed his name in soft exhale of breath that staggered him. Then she scooped her hands around to his chest and pushed his suit jacket down and off. Her fingers tore at the buttons of his shirt and he stepped back to help her, because she was taking too long and he needed to feel her skin flush with his. Shared heat, soft to hard, smooth to rough.

Yanking his shirt off, he laughed when she grinned, and a flash of something warm and hot and desperately dangerous pushed through him. She was more, so much more than great sex. So much more than the woman who carried his child. She was light and heat and smiles and laughter. She was everything he'd always dreamed of and everything he knew he couldn't have. And he wanted her more desperately than he'd ever wanted anything in his life.

He tore off the rest of his clothes, then grabbed her close again, sliding his hands up and down her body, pressing her tightly to him. "You feel so good," he murmured as he dipped his head to kiss the curve of her shoulder.

Her head fell back, exposing her throat, and she

said on a sigh, "You feel wonderful against me, Rick. I love it. I love how you kiss me." She lifted her head and met his gaze. Running her tongue across her bottom lip, she admitted, "I love how you feel inside me. I love what you make *me* feel."

His blood roared in his ears. Heart pounding against his chest, he couldn't breathe and didn't care. She was all that mattered. The next touch. The next kiss. The next taste of her.

He was hard and ready and wasn't willing to wait another second for her. Dragging her down to the lush carpet in front of the wide windows overlooking the strip, Rick scraped his hands up and down her body. He kissed her, plunging her depths, tasting, caressing, exploring her secrets and taking all she had to give.

Eileen held on tightly and met his tongue stroke for stroke. As his hands fired her blood and scorched her body, she planted her feet on the thick, soft carpet and lifted her hips in a silent plea. She wanted him within her. Needed to feel him fill her.

His hand swept down and cupped her and she groaned tightly, as tiny ripples of expectation shimmered through her. "Yes," she whispered, sliding her hands across his chest, smoothing, stroking. "Touch me, Rick. Touch me."

"Always," he murmured, and then he did. Dipping first one finger and then two into her depths, he stroked her, setting a rhythm that tantalized her even as he reached deeper and touched her soul. She felt the connection and hoped he felt it, too. Hoped he knew that she was giving him all that she was. Hoped he could believe in her.

And then her thoughts splintered as his thumb stroked her most sensitive spot. "Rick, I…need…"

"I know, baby," he whispered, his breath dusting warm across her face. "I know."

"Be in me," she said, and locked her gaze with his. "I need you to be inside me."

His jaw tightened, but he shifted, moving to cover her body with his and in seconds he was within her, claiming her, taking her higher, faster, than she'd ever been before. She moved with him, rocking her hips, finding the rhythm he set and she stared up into his eyes as the first explosion shuddered through her. Eileen called his name and held him tightly as she rode the wild wave of sensation cresting within. Moments later, he joined her and together they drifted slowly back to solid ground.

When the world stopped spinning and she thought she could gather enough breath to speak, Eileen said softly, "Happy wedding, Rick."

He lifted his head to stare down at her. "Same to you."

And if a small corner of her heart ached because she was in love with a man who would never believe that, she didn't let him know it.

Eleven

One month later, Eileen still wasn't sure if she'd done the right thing or not. Oh, she was married. She had pictures of the event to prove it.

She just wished she *felt* married.

But that wasn't easy when your brand-new husband insisted on treating you like a temporary roommate. A roommate he had great, amazing, mindboggling sex with, of course. But still, there was no closeness out of their bed. He was hardly ever at home, spending most of his days—even the weekends at his office. And she couldn't even see him there, since the temp agency had, true to their promise, sent a substitute secretary until Margo returned. Between Eileen's work at Larkspur and his hours at the office, the only time they ever saw each other was in bed. And once the sex was finished, he went to sleep, turning from her even as he prepared for her to leave him. There was no late-night cuddling and whispered conversations about the future. How could there be, she asked herself, if he didn't think they were going to *have* a future?

Eileen had tried to remain cheerful. She'd been right there, every day. Trying to prove to him that she wasn't leaving. But she could see it in his eyes that he didn't—or couldn't—trust her to stay.

"How's the new house coming?"

"What?"

"Hello?" Bridie grinned and grabbed a cookie for herself.

The scent of cinnamon sugar filled Bridie's kitchen and felt cozy and warm. As November drifted into December, the weather was cold and dreary, but being here, Eileen thought, really helped dispel the chill she carried inside her.

"Your new house," Bridie prodded. "How's it coming?"

The new house. Another sore spot. Eileen frowned. Rick had bought the huge Spanish-style house on a bluff overlooking Pacific Coast Highway without even consulting her. He said he'd wanted to surprise her. But the plain truth was, she thought, he was just trying to give her a gilded cage. By buying her a big house, he'd hoped to keep her there. To give her something she couldn't have gotten for herself.

But the house wasn't a home. It wasn't cozy and

small like her old cottage. It was empty and sterile and, so far, not exactly the land where dreams were made. She rattled around in the big place by herself more often than not and couldn't even convince him to help her pick out furniture.

"It's not," she finally said, blurting out the truth, before she could talk herself out of it.

"What do you mean?"

Eileen grabbed one of her sister's homemade snickerdoodle cookies and leaned back in her chair. "I mean, we don't even have any furniture. It looks like a warehouse. The few pieces I brought with me from the cottage hardly fill up a corner of it."

"For Pete's sake, Eileen. Take some time off work and furnish the place."

She crumbled the cookie slowly, watching each crumb drop to the table and bounce. "I don't want to do it alone, Bridie. It's *our* house. Or supposed to be. He should be a part of it."

"But..."

"But..." Eileen wanted to unload on her sister. God knows, she needed to talk to someone about this. But at the same time, she felt almost disloyal talking about Rick behind his back. Damn the man, couldn't he see that she loved him? Couldn't he see that he was pushing her away by not reaching out to her? Did he care?

As if sensing Eileen needed a change of subject, Bridie shifted gears. "I still can't believe you're married to my old boyfriend."

Eileen was grateful. She didn't want to think about her troubles right now. For this one moment, she wanted to enjoy being in her sister's happy home. This was what it should be like, she thought. This was how she and Rick should be living. With clutter and laughter and the sound of kids in the background. Instead, she had emptiness and silence.

Leaning forward, Eileen grabbed another cookie and this time she took a bite. "Gee thanks. What does that make Rick, the ultimate hand-me-down?"

Bridie's big blue eyes rolled. "Oh please. Let's see, he broke up with me in senior year of high school, so I'm thinking…*no.*"

"That's right," Eileen said, straightening in her chair as memories drifted through her mind like stray clouds across the sky. While her brain worked, her gaze shifted, scanning her sister's tidy blue-and-white kitchen as if looking for something. Idly she noted the kids' drawings stuck to the refrigerator doors, the small fingerprints left on the sliding glass door leading to the screened-in patio and crayons and coloring books scattered over the freshly waxed floor.

But she wasn't really seeing any of it. Instead, she was reaching back in her memory and discovering something she'd long forgotten. "You didn't break up with him, did you? *He* left you."

"Yeah," Bridie said. "And just before homecoming, too, the rat." Grinning, she added, "Lucky for him, I've decided to be a good sport and forgive him."

Excited, Eileen shook her head and leaned forward, bracing her arms on the polished oak table. "No, don't you get it? He broke up with you *before* you could break up with him."

Confusion filled her sister's eyes. "And this means...what, exactly?"

Eileen opened her mouth to speak but was cut off when a red-haired toddler burst into the room, tears streaking her tiny face.

"Mommy, Mommy," three-year-old Becky ran across the floor and slammed into her mother's right knee. "Jason won't let me fly with him."

"Honey, Jason can't fly. He—" Bridie's eyes widened as she jumped up. *"Fly?"* Already headed out to the backyard, she shouted, "Be back in a minute," and rushed out of the room.

Becky climbed up onto Eileen's lap, stole a cookie and leaned back against her. "Boys are dumb," she said around a bite of cookie.

Eileen stroked her niece's soft-as-silk hair and kissed the top of her head. "I'll remind you of that in about ten years."

But the little girl wasn't paying attention. She'd already slid off her aunt's lap and stretched out onto the floor, grabbing up her favorite purple crayon. While she watched her niece, Eileen smiled to herself, patted her abdomen and whispered, "No flying for you unless we're on a plane, deal?"

Then her smile slowly faded as thoughts of Rick poured back into her mind. Years ago, he'd broken up with Bridie to avoid having her break up with him. And Eileen had to wonder if his first marriage hadn't ended because he'd held back from Allison, too. Just as he was doing now, with her.

Oh, he hadn't actually *left* her. But he might as well have. He was hardly ever home—in that cavernous, impersonal house he'd bought for her. He kept himself at an emotional distance. He wouldn't be drawn into conversations. He didn't even want to talk about the baby or make plans, as if he already knew he wouldn't be a part of any plans Eileen might make.

He cared for her, she could see it in his eyes. He still turned to her at night, drawing her to him, giving her his body but not his heart. But otherwise, he moved like a ghost through her life.

There, but not connected.

Present, but not a part of anything.

Physically there, but emotionally distant.

He kept walls up around his heart in an attempt to protect it. But he didn't even realize that in building the walls, he was shutting love out, never letting it in. He was already cutting her out of his life so that when she left, he wouldn't be hurt.

And she didn't know if she could find a way past his defenses.

Two days later, nothing had changed and Eileen's legendary impatience was near implosion point. And she simply couldn't wait one more day to have her say. Waiting, trying her limited store of patience, wasn't helping. Maybe nothing would, a quiet, sad voice whispered in the back of her mind.

But she had to try.

And since he was leaving for a four day business trip to San Francisco, it was now...or wait some more.

She chose *now*.

Eileen was dressed and waiting in the kitchen when Rick came downstairs. She heard him long before she saw him, since his footsteps on the uncarpeted oak staircase echoed in the stillness.

The whole house was like an echo chamber. Wide front windows with a view of the ocean. Empty rooms. Unadorned floors. Nothing on the walls.

It felt abandoned.

She'd stewed about this for two days. Her dreams had been filled with it. And now it was time to make a stand. It was time to force Rick to talk to her. To make him see and admit, at least to himself, that he was shutting her out.

He came around the corner from the living room and stopped dead when he saw her. He wore a dark blue suit, pristine white shirt and a bloodred tie. His aftershave, a spicy mixture, drifted to her from across the room and she had to take a deep, calming breath to keep from rushing at him, throwing herself into his arms.

She knew he'd welcome her embrace.

There was nothing wrong with the physical side of their relationship, except for the fact that that was all they had going for them at the moment.

He set his garment bag down in the doorway, then shoved his hands into his pants pockets. "I thought you were going into the shop early today."

At least he listened to her when she talked. That was something.

"I called Paula," Eileen said. "She's going in to accept the deliveries." She took a long sip of her coffee, swallowed it, then set her cup on the counter. "I asked her to help me this morning, because I needed a few minutes with you before you left. We have to talk."

As if someone had hit a light switch, she actually *saw* those now-familiar shutters slam down over his eyes. He didn't have to physically back up for her to see him put more distance between them. "Can't," he said shortly. Checking his gold wristwatch briefly, he looked back at her. "Have to leave to catch my flight and—"

She interrupted his flow of excuses. They weren't good enough anymore, and she wouldn't let them stop her. "Rick, you can't just ignore me."

He walked past her toward the coffee pot. Pouring himself a half a cup, he glanced at her. "Nobody's ignoring you, Eileen."

He was so close his aftershave seemed to surround her. And yet, he was further away from her than ever. "Okay, poor choice of words." She reached up and tightened her ponytail before dropping her hands to the edge of the cold, gray—yes, *gray,* God, was everything in his world gray?—

granite counter. Steeling herself, she blurted, "You're not ignoring me. You're placating me."

"What?"

At least she had his attention. She swallowed hard. Now all she had to do was keep it. "This house for instance."

He took a drink. "I thought you liked the house."

"I do, but that's not the point."

He took another sip of his coffee and looked at her over the rim of the cup. "Then tell me what is."

Eileen just stared at him for a couple of heartbeats. Was he really that obtuse? "You bought this place without even telling me."

He stiffened slightly. "We already went over this. I wanted to surprise you."

Yeah, they'd gone over it. When she'd freaked out over his buying a house on a hill in Laguna as casually as most men bought a new shirt. She'd been bowled over by the beauty of it and hurt by the fact that he hadn't even included her in the decision to buy it. But it was hard to *stay* mad at a man for buying you a darn mansion. Even if she did miss the coziness of her cottage. "Congrats. It worked."

A muscle in his jaw twitched. "What're you getting at, Eyeball?"

The use of her old nickname should have warmed her. It didn't. It was simply something he tossed her, like throwing a hungry dog a meatless bone. He used it to pretend they were close. To somehow assure himself that everything was fine. It wasn't. She sighed, tipped her head back and looked him squarely in the eye. "We have to talk."

Rick's stomach fisted.

Every muscle in his body tightened as if waiting for a blow. He'd been expecting this. But even he was a little surprised that this moment had arrived only one short month after their wedding.

Watching her, his heart turned over. Her red-gold hair, in the ponytail she wore when she was going to work at her flower shop, swung like a metronome behind her head, ticking off her movements. It bounced when she walked and seemed to swing even harder when she was mad. It was a soft, shining indicator of her moods. And he loved the way it moved with her. She wore jeans and an old sweatshirt with a faded Santa lying in a recliner emblazoned across the front.

Everything about Eileen got to him.

Living with her, being with her all the time had been both heaven and hell. Hearing her voice in the darkness, having her no more than an arm's reach away during the long nights was more happiness than he'd ever known. She sang—badly—in the shower, cried at television commercials and thrived on the most appalling fast-food diet he'd ever seen. When happy, she laughed with a wholeheartedness that made him envy her joy. She'd stormed back into his life and turned it all upside down.

And realizing it was all going to end, knowing that she'd never stay, haunted him day and night.

He wanted to enjoy what time they might have

together, but every instinct kept urging him to pull back. To keep his heart distant. Safe. She smiled and he hungered for more. She sighed and turned into him in her sleep and his soul ached.

But if nothing else, her lack of interest in their home was the clincher for him. Eileen was a nester. Yet she hadn't done a damn thing in, or to, the house. No pictures on the walls, no pillows, no plants. Not even a bunch of flowers graced the sterile rooms. The monstrous house was exactly the opposite of her cozy cottage. She'd made it pretty clear that she considered this place a stopgap measure on her way to other things.

But if it was all going to end now, then he'd rather it was a clean break. He couldn't imagine a life now without her in it—didn't want to try—but if she was going, he thought, *go now*.

Before her leaving would kill him.

"Fine," he said, taking a deep gulp of coffee, letting the hot liquid burn his throat. That searing pain could at least distract him from the sound of his own heart breaking. "Talk."

"Wow." A breath shot from her lungs. "Feel the warmth."

His back teeth ground together. "Eileen…"

She held up one hand to silence him. "Are you my husband?"

"Excuse me?" Not the opener he was expecting.

"My husband," she repeated, and just for good measure, grabbed one of his hands and moved her fingers wildly in his palm as if using sign language to communicate. "Are you my husband, or are you just a close personal friend and a snuggling room-mate?"

He pulled his hand free of hers, then, with his hand at his side, he rubbed his fingers together, just to savor the warmth of her touch. "Where are you going with this?"

"No, the real question," she said, "is where have you been? Where are you now?"

Rick pushed away from the counter, needing to be mobile. "I'm standing right here. Being insulted."

Her face brightened, but there was no humor in her eyes. A sure sign that things were about to get rough. "Then this is an occasion! It's the first time you've been here. With *me*. Since we got married."

Okay, he wasn't going to take that. He was here. Day and night. He knew, because he'd gotten used to living with tension as white-hot as a live electrical wire. "What're you talking about? We both live here."

"No," she countered with a slow shake of her head that sent her ponytail into a wide wave. "*I* live here. You just haunt the place."

Stalking past him, she crossed the kitchen floor, her heels clacking on the terra-cotta tile. That ponytail swung back and forth furiously and, despite the anger churning in the room, Rick couldn't keep his gaze off it. When she whirled around to face him, the emotion in her eyes tore at him.

Then she spoke and for a minute he was lost.

"You broke up with Bridie."

He stared at her for a long moment, then shook his head as if to clear it. How'd they get from talking about *them* to talking about his breakup with her sister more than ten years ago? *"What?"*

"My sister. Bridget."

"I *know* who Bridie is," he snapped. "What I don't get, is what the hell you're talking about."

"You really don't, do you?" she asked, anger sliding from her as easily as rainwater rolling down a glass window pane.

"Enlighten me."

"Gladly." She planted both hands at her hips and met his glare without flinching. "Your senior year, you broke up with Bridie right before homecoming."

"And this is important…why?"

She smiled, but it was a sad, small twist of her lips that tugged at his heart. "God, Rick. You were doing it back then too, and you still don't realize it."

There was only so much psychoanalyzing he was willing to put up with. "I don't know what you're talking about," he said, walking to the sink to set his coffee cup down on the shining, cold stainless steel.

"You broke up with Bridie to keep *her* from breaking up with *you*."

Something pinged inside him. Recognition?

No.

"I broke up with Bridie because I couldn't afford a girlfriend."

"No, you couldn't," she said, her voice a low, strained whisper. "Just like you can't *afford* a wife, now."

He snapped her a look, then slowly turned to face her. "You've got me all figured out," he said quietly. "Let's hear it."

"Okay." She shoved her hands into her jeans pockets and rocked back and forth, her tennis shoes squeaking on the clean tiles. "You were afraid of caring too much for Bridie, so you broke up with her." Just like now, you're terrified to love me, so you pretend I'm not here."

"That's it." That was a little too close to home. His insides twisted into knots and his heart ached as though a giant fist was squeezing it. Rick held up both hands. "I don't have time for this. We'll talk when I get back from San Francisco."

She stepped in front of him when he crossed the room to pick up his garment bag. Pulling her hands free of her jeans, she slapped both palms against his chest to stop him. "No, we won't talk—because you *don't* talk."

"Yeah?" he countered, trying not to feel the warmth of her hands, spreading down, into the chill of his soul. "What do you call *this?* What we're doing now?"

She ignored that.

"This isn't right," she said. "It isn't enough."

"What's not enough?" he spoke up quickly,

fighting a losing battle yet unable to surrender just yet. "I married you. Committed to you."

"You won't even commit to a *couch,* Rick."

He reached up and scraped both hands through his hair. "I told you, buy the damn furniture. Get whatever you want. You have the credit cards, go crazy."

She gave him a shove that didn't budge him an inch, then dropped her hands and stepped back. "Don't you get it? This is supposed to be *our* house. If I furnish it, it's *my* house. I want you *here,* Rick. I want this place—*me*—to matter."

"Damn it, Eileen, you *do* matter. You're carrying my child."

A short, harsh laugh shot from her throat as a single tear escaped her eye and rolled down her cheek. "This isn't about the baby. This is about *us.* Or the us we might have been."

Cold radiated from his heart and spilled throughout his bloodstream. He just managed to keep from shivering in reaction. "God. You're telling me we go from no furniture to divorce court?"

Sadly she shook her head and wiped away her tears with an impatient swipe of her hands. "The empty house is a metaphor. Don't you understand? Don't you see? *We're* empty, too, Rick. And we always will be until you let me in. But you won't do that, will you?"

He reached out to her, then let his hand drop to his side, his fingers curling tightly into a helpless fist. Holding her wasn't the answer, because he could never hold her tightly enough to keep her. Heart aching, breath strangling in his chest, Rick muttered thickly, "Can we just talk about this when I get back?"

"Heck, why bother to come back, Rick? Why should *I* be here?" She looked up into his eyes and Rick felt himself falling into those green depths and wanted, desperately, to let himself go. To give in to the need to be a part of her. To be held deep within her body, her heart. To finally find a place—a heart—he could call home. But pain was a good teacher and it held him tight in its grip. Memories flooded his brain, reminding him just what it was like to lose the very thing you valued most. And that reminder was enough to keep him from reaching for her, burying his face in the curve of her neck, inhaling the sweet, floral scent of her.

"This is an empty house, Rick," she said, her voice low and harsh, as though she were having to push each word past a throat clogged with emotion. "And it'll always *be* empty because that's the way *you* want it."

He flinched as if she'd struck him. But this blow was sharper, deeper than if she'd slapped his face. That would only have been physical. This cut him right down to his bones.

"You don't want to take a chance," she said, reaching around him to pluck her car keys off the counter. "You *want* to shut yourself off until no one can reach you." Her gaze locked on him again and he read the sorrow written there. "Well, that's safe," she said, "but it's lonely as hell. Are you *trying* to be alone for the rest of your life?"

All Rick heard was her saying *Why should I be here?* She was leaving, then. Just as he'd known she would. It was over. And why did it hurt so much? Why was pain radiating through his body with strength enough to cripple him? He'd protected himself to prevent this much pain. He'd held back. Hadn't admitted even to himself just how much he cared.

And now he never would.

He'd never let himself think the word *love,* because knowing he'd loved her and lost her...would finish him off.

She turned then and headed for the front door.

Rick followed after her, listening to the sound of her footsteps pounding through the silence like a heartbeat frantically beating its last.

She had stepped through the front door and was halfway down the walk before he spoke.

"I *knew* you'd leave."

Twelve

In her car, Eileen slapped the dashboard, completely disgusted with herself. "Damn it. I *did* leave!" She'd fallen right into his expectations. Done exactly what he'd believed from the first that she would do. She'd fulfilled his predictions, despite her intentions. "I can't believe it. What was I thinking?"

Naturally she didn't have an answer to her own idiocy. She reached up and scrubbed both hands over her face as if she could wipe away the memory of the last few minutes. "I walked out on him. Left him standing in that big, empty house all alone. Stupid, stupid, stupid."

Gran used to say that one day her impatience would get the better of her. Well, as much as it irked her to admit it, Gran had been right. She'd given in to her frustration, her fury and she couldn't take any of it back now. Even if she tried, he'd never believe her.

From now on, every time he looked at her, he'd see her walking away from him and he'd never stop waiting for it to happen again.

It didn't really matter whether she'd had reason enough to do it or not.

She shouldn't have walked out.

But as long as she had, she wouldn't go rushing back in all apologies and promises. She'd already made a promise to him. At their wedding. But he hadn't believed that one, so why would he believe one now?

No. She'd sit here a minute or two. Wait. See if he came after her. If he was willing to fight for her. For *them.*

Seconds crawled past and stretched into minutes and the only sound was her own breathing and the wind pushing at the car.

He wasn't coming.

And she couldn't go back inside.

Not now.

"For Pete's sake, Eileen," she snapped as she fired up the ignition and gave the house one last look. "You *married* him, hoping to teach him you *wouldn't* leave." She threw the Jeep into first gear. As she pulled out of the driveway and turned into the street, she muttered, "Nice job."

* * *

On the last night of his business trip, Rick was like a man possessed. He couldn't keep his mind on the job. Didn't have the patience to deal with crotchety clients only worried about the fluctuations in the market.

"What the hell does the market matter?" he groused as he flopped onto the hotel bed and reached for the phone. "Nothing matters," he said, answering his own question as he got an outside line and punched in the phone number to the big house in Laguna. "Nothing matters but Eileen."

He'd been gone four days. And wondering where she was. What she was doing. What she was thinking. Because he'd done a hell of a lot of thinking since she'd walked out the door that last morning.

She was right.

About everything.

He'd broken up with Bridie and others like her, over the years, to prevent *them* from breaking up with *him*. It was a pattern he hadn't even seen. It hadn't made sense then. Or now, for that matter. But he didn't want to make the same mistake again—not when, this time, there was so much more riding on it than a homecoming dance.

Over and over again, his brain had replayed the image of Eileen striding away from him. Again and again he heard the sound of her car's engine firing up.

He hadn't gone after her.

He'd stood there, stupidly watching her drive off. Yet…in his dreams, it was different. In his dreams, he'd chased after her. He'd caught her before she opened the car door. He'd pulled her into his arms and told her he loved her. Asked her to stay. Asked her to love him. To be with him. To never leave.

And in his dreams, she smiled.

And came back to him.

But dreams weren't reality and when he woke, he was in a hotel. Alone.

Across the room, the muted television flickered wildly, and light played in the shadows of his otherwise darkened hotel room.

He listened as the phone in the empty house on the bluff rang and rang and rang. She wasn't there. She'd left and she wasn't coming back. He could picture the empty house. The big rooms. The silence. And he knew that without Eileen in his life, no matter where he lived, he would be surrounded by emptiness. Silence would follow him through the years. He would watch his child grow up with the love of its mother and Rick would know, always, that he might have shared in it all. Might have been a part of something wonderful. Instead, he would be on the outside, as he'd always been, looking at love, wanting it, but never having it.

And always knowing that it could have been different, if he hadn't been too much of a coward to take a risk with his heart.

He hung up, setting the receiver back into its cradle. Then, looking into the mirror over the generically ugly dresser, he stared into his own eyes and said, "So what're you gonna do about it, you idiot?"

No-brainer.

Hopping off the bed, he stalked to the closet, snatched up his suitcase and started throwing things into it. With any luck, he could catch an early flight home. And if his luck was *very* good...he'd find Eileen still willing to talk.

It was raining.

Her car was in the driveway.

Rick's heartbeat sputtered erratically as the windshield wipers pushed at the sheet of water crashing onto the car. He stared at a blurred image of her jeep and told himself not to get his hopes up. He hadn't expected to find her here. He'd thought he'd have to track her down at Larkspur and somehow *force* her to listen to him.

But this was better.

He should tell her here, in the place he'd wanted them to call home.

Pulling in behind her, he parked his car, jumped out and ran to the front door. By the time he hit the front porch, he was drenched. He could hardly breathe. Desperation fueled him. He knew now. He could admit it now. When it was too late, he could finally make himself say it and believe it. He loved her. Completely. And this was perhaps his last chance to convince her of that.

He unlocked the door and stepped into a strange place.

Standing on the marble tiles in the foyer, Rick swiped his soaking wet hair off his forehead and out of his eyes. Quietly he closed the door behind him, without ever taking his gaze off the room in front of him.

Area rugs were sprinkled across the wide expanse of knotty pine flooring. Lamps stood on highly polished oak tables, sending puddles of golden light into the room, banishing the shadows. A fire burned in the wide, stone hearth, flames snapping and dancing across the wood stacked behind a black wrought-iron screen. Two floral-patterned sofas in a dark burgundy fabric sat facing each other, with a huge oak table supporting a bowl of fresh flowers between them.

Paintings, dozens of them, hung on the walls and under the wide front windows stood a multitiered plant stand boasting ferns and flowered plants that spilled onto the floor.

Rick held his breath, tears sheening his vision until he blinked them back and rubbed one hand across his mouth. He took one hesitant step into the room, almost afraid to move, lest it all be an hallucination that would dissolve on his moving.

But it remained.

All of it.

From the kitchen, the delicious scent of bubbling pasta sauce reached for him. His mouth watered. But it wasn't the promise of food delighting him.

It was the promise of so much more.

But where was Eileen?

He stopped to listen, straining to hear something that would lead him to her. And that's when he heard it. A radio, playing softly. Old Blue Eyes was crooning about a summer wind.

Leaving a trail of water in his wake, Rick headed for the stairs, and before he'd taken more than two steps he was running. He hit the first carpeted tread and, grinning, he grabbed the banister and kept running, taking the stairs two and three at a time.

In the long hall, he kept moving. Blood racing, heart pounding, head spinning. He glanced into rooms as he passed and where there was once just cavernous, empty places, there was now, a *home*. Fresh flowers everywhere, there was furniture and rugs and paintings and…everything he'd hoped for. Everything he'd ever wanted.

And following the sound of the music, he stopped at the threshold of the nursery and saw the woman who had given it all to him, despite his own stupidity. Her back to him, she swayed to the music and the crooner's smooth-as-silk voice. Rick's heartbeat steadied, but he felt that organ swell to the point of bursting as he looked around the room where his child would live. Clouds dotted the blue ceiling. A mural of a garden colored one wall and the white furniture was offset by the multicolored linens and the pillows tucked into a rocking chair just waiting for a mother and her child.

"You came back."

She stopped struggling to hang the picture of a mother bunny and looked over her shoulder at him.

"Boy, am I glad to see you," she said with a grin. "I need a tall person to hang this."

His throat closed and, instead of trying to speak, Rick walked across the room, took the picture from her and carefully hung it from the nail in the wall.

"There. Finished." She looked up at him. "Doesn't it look great?"

"Great doesn't even come close," he murmured, and grabbed her. "You're here. I can't believe you're here. God, Eileen. I need you so much. I—" Pulling her to him, he enfolded her in his arms and held on tight, just in case she might change her mind at the last minute and make a run for the door.

He couldn't hold her tightly enough. Couldn't feel her close enough. And he suspected he'd never be able to hold her tight enough to satisfy all of the hungers within him.

She hugged him, then pulled her head back to look up at him. "Surprised?"

Scooping one hand up to cup her cheek, Rick let his gaze move over her, assuring himself that she was real—and here—in his arms. "Oh, yeah."

"Good. Then my work here is done."

One brief flash of panic flared inside him. "Don't leave."

"What?"

"Don't leave, Eyeball. Don't ever leave me."

"I'm not going anywhere, Rick," she said, and her voice softened on the tears clouding her eyes. "I love you, you big dummy."

He laughed and it felt good. Everything felt good.

For days, he'd held his pain close. Nurturing it. Telling himself it was what it was. But now, as he looked into her eyes and saw the love shining there, he knew pain would never be able to touch him again.

"I love you," he said, and waited a beat for the words to register in her eyes. "I'm not afraid to say it anymore. But I was. God, Eileen. I thought I loved you too much."

She smiled up at him and his world straightened up and felt right again.

"There's never too much love."

"I think I know that now," he said. "But I just love you so much it terrified me to think of losing you. And God, then I almost chased you away."

She shook her head and held his face between her palms. "Not a chance, Rick. I'm not going anywhere."

"I know," he said, feeling years of cold drift away in the rush of warmth spilling into his soul. "I knew the minute I saw the house. What you'd done to it. And a part of me knew before. I was just too scared to believe." His hands moved up and down her arms, and back up to her face, her hair. He couldn't seem to touch her enough.

"I called here last night. I wanted to talk to you— needed to talk to you—but no one answered and I—"

She placed her fingers across his mouth. "They painted the nursery yesterday and the smell made me sick, so I stayed at Gran's."

"The nursery," he repeated, savoring the words. The images they painted. He and Eileen. Their child. And the others that would follow. He could see them now, moving through the years together.

And he thanked God for granting a fool one more chance at love.

Eileen lifted her arms to encircle his neck and, smiling up at him, she said softly, "Welcome home, Rick. Welcome home."

Then she kissed him and Rick knew that at last he'd finally found home. Here, with Eileen, his temporary secretary and forever love.

Epilogue

Five years later...

"**D**addy, where's mommy?"

"Shh," Rick whispered as his four-year-old son Ryan climbed up onto the couch beside him. "You'll wake the baby."

Ryan reached out one chubby hand to pat the infant asleep and sprawled across her daddy's chest. "Kerry's not sleepin'."

"She will be if we're quiet," Rick said, smoothing his son's hair back off his sweaty forehead. The little boy had been running all over the backyard with his puppy until the little dog lay in a crumpled heap of exhaustion on the rug. Ryan, however, was harder to exhaust. His other sister Katie, two years old and a bigger handful than her older brother had *ever* been, was, thankfully, fast asleep in her room upstairs.

And if Rick could just get Ryan to lower his voice, he had high hopes for getting Kerry down for a nap, too. But at six months old, the baby was determined to not miss a thing and rarely closed her big green eyes.

In a stage whisper that could have been heard from outside, Ryan leaned in and asked, "When's Mommy comin' back?"

"In a while," Rick told him and felt love rush into his heart for this child and the others he and Eileen had been blessed with. He had so much now. So very much. "She went shopping, remember?"

"To buy me somethin'?" Ryan flopped into Rick's side and idly played with his sister's tiny hand.

"Probably," Rick admitted, smiling. With Christmas right around the corner, Eileen had taken off for some quality time at the mall with her sister. But Rick didn't mind. There was just nothing he liked better than being with his family.

"When's she comin', though?" Ryan tipped his head back to look up at his daddy. "Are we worried?"

Rick leaned over and kissed the top of his dark blond head. "No, we're not worried," he said, smiling. "Mommy's having fun with aunt Bridie."

Ryan nodded. "Cousin Jason says he's gonna teach me to fly."

Rick rolled his eyes and made a mental note to talk to his nephew. "No flying for you, buddy. Okay?"

"'kay. When's Mommy comin'?"

Rick sighed and Kerry squirmed on his chest, lifted her head and gave him a drooly smile that tugged at his heart. "So much for nap time, huh?" he asked, laughing just as the sound of a car engine came to him. "Hey, bud. Mommy's home."

"Yay!" Ryan shrieked, jumped off the couch and clattered across the floor to the front door. Rick was just a step or two behind him, cradling his now wide-awake infant daughter in his arms.

He opened the door and watched Ryan race outside to greet his mother. It was enough for Rick to stand on the porch and watch that gorgeous redhead climb out of her Jeep and scoop her son up into her arms for a big kiss. In a splash of sunlight, she turned and grinned at him and Rick counted his blessings again.

"Hey," Eileen called out, "I need some help with these bags."

He nodded and walked down the steps to join her. Handing her the baby, Rick leaned in for a quick kiss.

"Miss me?" she teased, smoothing the baby's wispy red-gold hair back from her forehead.

"Always," he said.

"But we wasn't worried," Ryan chimed in.

"No?" she asked, still smiling.

"No," Ryan said with confidence, "cause my daddy says that Mommy's always come home."

Eileen's features softened and her mouth curved as Rick leaned in for another kiss. Their mouths met in a promise of more to come later.

Then, with his son tugging at his pants leg, Rick winked and said quietly, "Welcome home, Eyeball."

*   *   *   *   *

Silhouette
Desire

From acclaimed author
CINDY GERARD
Tempting the Tycoon
(Silhouette Desire #1539)

As the wedding coordinator at a glitzy Palm Beach hotel, Rachel Matthews has made a living out of making other women's happily-ever-afters come true. But as far as this lovelorn career woman is concerned, she won't be planning her own bash *anytime* soon. But then all bets are off when she catches the appreciative gaze of hotshot millionaire Nate McGrory....

You won't want to miss this brand-new tale that's brimming with steamy sensuality, heightened emotion... and intoxicating romance!

Available October 2003 at your favorite retail outlet.

Visit Silhouette at www.eHarlequin.com   SDTTT

Your opinion is important to us! Please take a few moments to share your thoughts with us about your experiences with Harlequin and Silhouette books. Your comments will be very useful in ensuring that we deliver books you love to read.
Please take a few minutes to complete the questionnaire, then send it to us at the address below.

Send your completed questionnaires to:
Harlequin/Silhouette Reader Survey, P.O. Box 9046, Buffalo, NY 14269-9046

1. As you may know, there are many different lines under the Harlequin and Silhouette brands. Each of the lines is listed below. Please check the box that most represents your reading habit for each line.

Line	Currently read this line	Do not read this line	Not sure if I read this line
Harlequin American Romance	❏	❏	❏
Harlequin Duets	❏	❏	❏
Harlequin Romance	❏	❏	❏
Harlequin Historicals	❏	❏	❏
Harlequin Superromance	❏	❏	❏
Harlequin Intrigue	❏	❏	❏
Harlequin Presents	❏	❏	❏
Harlequin Temptation	❏	❏	❏
Harlequin Blaze	❏	❏	❏
Silhouette Special Edition	❏	❏	❏
Silhouette Romance	❏	❏	❏
Silhouette Intimate Moments	❏	❏	❏
Silhouette Desire	❏	❏	❏

2. Which of the following best describes why you bought *this book?* One answer only, please.

the picture on the cover	❏	the title	❏
the author	❏	the line is one I read often	❏
part of a miniseries	❏	saw an ad in another book	❏
saw an ad in a magazine/newsletter	❏	a friend told me about it	❏
I borrowed/was given this book	❏	other: _____	❏

3. Where did you buy *this book?* One answer only, please.

at Barnes & Noble	❏	at a grocery store	❏
at Waldenbooks	❏	at a drugstore	❏
at Borders	❏	on eHarlequin.com Web site	❏
at another bookstore	❏	from another Web site	❏
at Wal-Mart	❏	Harlequin/Silhouette Reader	
at Target	❏	Service/through the mail	❏
at Kmart	❏	used books from anywhere	❏
at another department store or mass merchandiser	❏	I borrowed/was given this book	❏

4. On average, how many Harlequin and Silhouette books do you buy at one time?

I buy _____ books at one time	❏
I rarely buy a book	❏

MRQ403SD-1A

5. How many times per month do you shop for any *Harlequin and/or Silhouette* books?
One answer only, please.

1 or more times a week	❑	a few times per year	❑
1 to 3 times per month	❑	less often than once a year	❑
1 to 2 times every 3 months	❑	never	❑

6. When you think of your ideal heroine, which *one* statement describes her the best?
One answer only, please.

She's a woman who is strong-willed	❑	She's a desirable woman	❑
She's a woman who is needed by others	❑	She's a powerful woman	❑
She's a woman who is taken care of	❑	She's a passionate woman	❑
She's an adventurous woman	❑	She's a sensitive woman	❑

7. The following statements describe types or genres of books that you may be
interested in reading. Pick *up to 2 types* of books that you are most interested in.

I like to read about truly romantic relationships	❑
I like to read stories that are sexy romances	❑
I like to read romantic comedies	❑
I like to read a romantic mystery/suspense	❑
I like to read about romantic adventures	❑
I like to read romance stories that involve family	❑
I like to read about a romance in times or places that I have never seen	❑
Other: _____	❑

*The following questions help us to group your answers with those readers who are
similar to you. Your answers will remain confidential.*

8. Please record your year of birth below.

19 ____

9. What is your marital status?

single ❑   married ❑   common-law ❑   widowed ❑
divorced/separated ❑

10. Do you have children 18 years of age or younger currently living at home?

yes ❑   no ❑

11. Which of the following best describes your employment status?

employed full-time or part-time ❑   homemaker ❑   student ❑
retired ❑   unemployed ❑

12. Do you have access to the Internet from either home or work?

yes ❑   no ❑

13. Have you ever visited eHarlequin.com?

yes ❑   no ❑

14. What state do you live in?

_____

15. Are you a member of Harlequin/Silhouette Reader Service?

yes ❑   Account # _____   no ❑   MRQ403SD-1B

Is your man too good to be true?

Hot, gorgeous AND romantic?
If so, he could be a Harlequin® Blaze™ series cover model!

Our grand-prize winners will receive a trip for two to New York City to
shoot the cover of a Blaze novel, and will stay at the luxurious Plaza Hotel.
Plus, they'll receive $500 U.S. spending money!
The runner-up winners will receive $200 U.S.
to spend on a romantic dinner for two.

It's easy to enter!

In 100 words or less, tell us what makes your boyfriend or spouse a true romantic
and the perfect candidate for the cover of a Blaze novel, and include in your submission
two photos of this potential cover model.

All entries must include the written submission of the contest entrant, two photographs of the model
candidate and the Official Entry Form and Publicity Release forms completed in full and signed by
both the model candidate and the contest entrant. Harlequin, along with the experts at
Elite Model Management, will select a winner.

For photo and complete Contest details, please refer to the Official Rules on the next page. All entries
will become the property of Harlequin Enterprises Ltd. and are not returnable.

**Please visit www.blazecovermodel.com to download a copy of the Official Entry Form and
Publicity Release Form or send a request to one of the addresses below.**

Please mail your entry to: **Harlequin Blaze Cover Model Search**

In U.S.A.
P.O. Box 9069
Buffalo, NY
14269-9069

In Canada
P.O. Box 637
Fort Erie, ON
L2A 5X3

No purchase necessary. Contest open to Canadian and U.S. residents who are 18 and over.
Void where prohibited. Contest closes September 30, 2003.

HARLEQUIN® *Blaze*™

HBCVRMODEL1

HARLEQUIN BLAZE COVER MODEL SEARCH CONTEST 3569 OFFICIAL RULES
NO PURCHASE NECESSARY TO ENTER

1. To enter, submit two (2) 4" x 6" photographs of a boyfriend or spouse (who must be 18 years of age or older) taken no later than three (3) months from the time of entry: a close-up, waist up, shirtless photograph; and a fully clothed, full-length photograph, then, tell us, in 100 words or fewer, why he should be a Harlequin Blaze cover model and how he is romantic. Your complete "entry" must include: (i) your essay, (ii) the Official Entry Form and Publicity Release Form printed below completed and signed by you (as "Entrant"), (iii) the photographs (with your hand-written name, address and phone number, and your model's name, address and phone number on the back of each photograph), and (iv) the Publicity Release Form and Photograph Representation Form printed below completed and signed by your model (as "Model"), and should be sent via first-class mail to either: Harlequin Blaze Cover Model Search Contest 3569, P.O. Box 9069, Buffalo, NY, 14269-9069, or Harlequin Blaze Cover Model Search Contest 3569, P.O. Box 637, Fort Erie, Ontario L2A 5X3. All submissions must be in English and be received no later than September 30, 2003. Limit: one entry per person, household or organization. **Purchase or acceptance of a product offer does not improve your chances of winning.** All entry requirements must be strictly adhered to for eligibility and to ensure fairness among entries.

2. Ten (10) Finalist submissions (photographs and essays) will be selected by a panel of judges consisting of members of the Harlequin editorial, marketing and public relations staff, as well as a representative from Elite Model Management (Toronto) Inc., based on the following criteria:

Aptness/Appropriateness of submitted photographs for a Harlequin Blaze cover—70%
Originality of Essay—20%
Sincerity of Essay—10%

In the event of a tie, duplicate finalists will be selected. The photographs submitted by finalists will be posted on the Harlequin website no later than November 15, 2003 (at www.blazecovermodel.com), and viewers may vote, in rank order, on their favorite(s) to assist in the panel of judges' final determination of the Grand Prize and Runner-up winning entries based on the above judging criteria. All decisions of the judges are final.

3. All entries become the property of Harlequin Enterprises Ltd. and none will be returned. Any entry may be used for future promotional purposes. Elite Model Management (Toronto) Inc. and/or its partners, subsidiaries and affiliates operating as "Elite Model Management" will have access to all entries including all personal information, and may contact any Entrant and/or Model in its sole discretion for their own business purposes. Harlequin and Elite Model Management (Toronto) Inc. are separate entities with no legal association or partnership whatsoever having no power to bind or obligate the other or create any expressed or implied obligation or responsibility on behalf of the other, such that Harlequin shall not be responsible in any way for any acts or omissions of Elite Model Management (Toronto) Inc. or its partners, subsidiaries and affiliates in connection with the Contest or otherwise and Elite Model Management shall not be responsible in any way for any acts or omissions of Harlequin or its partners, subsidiaries and affiliates in connection with the contest or otherwise.

4. All Entrants and Models must be residents of the U.S. or Canada, be 18 years of age or older, and have no prior criminal convictions. The contest is not open to any Model that is a professional model and/or actor in any capacity at the time of the entry. Contest void wherever prohibited by law; all applicable laws and regulations apply. Any litigation within the Province of Quebec regarding the conduct or organization of a publicity contest may be submitted to the Régie des alcools, des courses et des jeux for a ruling, and any litigation regarding the awarding of a prize may be submitted to the Régie only for the purpose of helping the parties reach a settlement. Employees and immediate family members of Harlequin Enterprises Ltd., D.L. Blair, Inc., Elite Model Management (Toronto) Inc. and their parents, affiliates, subsidiaries and all other agencies, entities and persons connected with the use, marketing or conduct of this Contest are not eligible to enter. Acceptance of any prize offered constitutes permission to use Entrants' and Models' names, essay submissions, photographs or other likenesses for the purposes of advertising, trade, publication and promotion on behalf of Harlequin Enterprises Ltd., its parent, affiliates, subsidiaries, assigns and other authorized entities involved in the judging and promotion of the contest without further compensation to any Entrant or Model, unless prohibited by law.

5. Finalists will be determined no later than October 30, 2003. Prize Winners will be determined no later than January 31, 2004. Grand Prize Winners (consisting of winning Entrant and Model) will be required to sign and return Affidavit of Eligibility/Release of Liability and Model Release forms within thirty (30) days of notification. Non-compliance with this requirement and within the specified time period will result in disqualification and an alternate will be selected. Any prize notification returned as undeliverable will result in the awarding of the prize to an alternate set of winners. All travelers (or parent/legal guardian of a minor) must execute the Affidavit of Eligibility/Release of Liability prior to ticketing and must possess required travel documents (e.g. valid photo ID) where applicable. Travel dates specified by Sponsor but no later than May 30, 2004.

6. Prizes: One (1) Grand Prize—the opportunity for the Model to appear on the cover of a paperback book from the Harlequin Blaze series, and a 3 day/2 night trip for two (Entrant and Model) to New York, NY for the photo shoot of Model which includes round-trip coach air transportation from the commercial airport nearest the winning Entrant's home to New York, NY, (or, in lieu of air transportation, $100 cash payable to Entrant and Model, if the winning Entrant's home is within 250 miles of New York, NY), hotel accommodations (double occupancy) at the Plaza Hotel and $500 cash spending money payable to Entrant and Model, (approximate prize value: $8,000), and one (1) Runner-up Prize of $200 cash payable to Entrant and Model for a romantic dinner for two (approximate prize value: $200). Prizes are valued in U.S. currency. Prizes consist of only those items listed as part of the prize. No substitution of prize(s) permitted by winners. All prizes are awarded jointly to the Entrant and Model of the winning entries, and are not severable - prizes and obligations may not be assigned or transferred. Any change to the Entrant and/or Model of the winning entries will result in disqualification and an alternate will be selected. Taxes on prize are the sole responsibility of winners. Any and all expenses and/or items not specifically described as part of the prize are the sole responsibility of winners. Harlequin Enterprises Ltd. and D.L. Blair, Inc., their parents, affiliates, and subsidiaries are not responsible for errors in printing of Contest entries and/or game pieces. No responsibility is assumed for lost, stolen, late, illegible, incomplete, inaccurate, non-delivered, postage due or misdirected mail or entries. In the event of printing or other errors which may result in unintended prize values or duplication of prizes, all affected game pieces or entries shall be null and void.

7. Winners will be notified by mail. For winners' list (available after March 31, 2004), send a self-addressed, stamped envelope to: Harlequin Blaze Cover Model Search Contest 3569 Winners, P.O. Box 4200, Blair, NE 68009-4200, or refer to the Harlequin website (at www.blazecovermodel.com).

Contest sponsored by Harlequin Enterprises Ltd., P.O. Box 9042, Buffalo, NY 14269-9042.

HBCVRMODEL2

If you enjoyed what you just read,
then we've got an offer you can't resist!

Take 2 bestselling love stories FREE!

Plus get a FREE surprise gift!

Clip this page and mail it to Silhouette Reader Service™

IN U.S.A.	**IN CANADA**
3010 Walden Ave.	P.O. Box 609
P.O. Box 1867	Fort Erie, Ontario
Buffalo, N.Y. 14240-1867	L2A 5X3

YES! Please send me 2 free Silhouette Desire® novels and my free surprise gift. After receiving them, if I don't wish to receive anymore, I can return the shipping statement marked cancel. If I don't cancel, I will receive 6 brand-new novels every month, before they're available in stores! In the U.S.A., bill me at the bargain price of $3.57 plus 25¢ shipping and handling per book and applicable sales tax, if any*. In Canada, bill me at the bargain price of $4.24 plus 25¢ shipping and handling per book and applicable taxes**. That's the complete price and a savings of at least 10% off the cover prices—what a great deal! I understand that accepting the 2 free books and gift places me under no obligation ever to buy any books. I can always return a shipment and cancel at any time. Even if I never buy another book from Silhouette, the 2 free books and gift are mine to keep forever.

225 SDN DNUP
326 SDN DNUQ

Name	(PLEASE PRINT)	
Address	Apt.#	
City	State/Prov.	Zip/Postal Code

* Terms and prices subject to change without notice. Sales tax applicable in N.Y.
** Canadian residents will be charged applicable provincial taxes and GST.
All orders subject to approval. Offer limited to one per household and not valid to current Silhouette Desire® subscribers.
® are registered trademarks of Harlequin Books S.A., used under license.

DES02 ©1998 Harlequin Enterprises Limited

COMING NEXT MONTH

#1537 MAN IN CONTROL—Diana Palmer
Long, Tall Texans
Undercover agent Alexander Cobb joined forces with his sworn enemy Jodie Clayburn to crack a case. Surprisingly, working together proved to be the easy part. The trouble they faced was fighting the fiery attraction that threatened to consume them both!

#1538 BORN TO BE WILD—Anne Marie Winston
Dynasties: The Barones
Celia Papleo had been just a girl when Reese Barone sailed out of her life, leaving her heart shattered. But now she was all woman—and more than a match for the wealthy man who tempted her again. Could a night of passion erase the misunderstandings of the past?

#1539 TEMPTING THE TYCOON—Cindy Gerard
Helping women find their happily-ever-afters was wedding planner Rachel Matthew's trade. But she refused to risk her own heart. That didn't stop roguishly charming millionaire lawyer Nate McGrory from wanting to claim her for himself…and envisioning her icy facade turing to molten lava at his touch!

#1540 LONETREE RANCHERS: MORGAN—Kathie DeNosky
Owning the most successful ranch in Wyoming was Morgan Wakefield's dream. And it was now within his grasp—as long as he wed Samantha Peterson. Their marriage was strictly a business arrangement—but it didn't stem the desire they felt when together….

#1541 HAVING THE BEST MAN'S BABY—Shawna Delacorte
For Jean Summerfield, the one thing worse than having to wear a bridesmaid dress was facing her unreliable ex, best man Ry Collier. But Jean's dormant desire sparked to life at Ry's touch. Would Ry stay to face the consequences of their passion, or leave her burned once more?

#1542 COWBOY'S MILLION-DOLLAR SECRET—Emilie Rose
Charismatic cowboy Patrick Lander knew exactly who he was—until virginal beauty Leanna Jensen brought news that Patrick would inherit his biological father's multimillion-dollar estate! The revelation threw Patrick's settled life into chaos—but paled compared to the emotions Leanna aroused in him.

SDCNM0903